ALSO

Seven Range Shifters

Cowboy Wolf Trouble

Cowboy in Wolf's Clothing

Wicked Cowboy Wolf

Fierce Cowboy Wolf

Wild Cowboy Wolf

Cowboy Wolf Outlaw

The Rogue Brotherhood

Rogue Wolf Hunter

COWBOY WOLF CHRISTMAS

KAIT BALLENGER

Copyright © 2022 by Kait Ballenger

All rights reserved.

No part of this book may be reproduced in any form or by any electronic or mechanical means, including information storage and retrieval systems, without written permission from the author, except for the use of brief quotations in a book review.

For Mara
for helping me see myself in these pages

*We want readers to be well-informed.
If you would like to know if this book has any elements of concern for you, please check the author's website for details:
www.kaitballenger.com*

1

Was it too much to ask for a bit of peace? Silas Buck snarled as he prowled through the snow, clutching his leather Stetson against the harsh, whistling winds. The blue-ridged Montana mountains loomed in the distance, their frozen peaks barely visible against the blinding snow which now coated the ranchlands, until nothing but a stretch of endless white remained. There were only three days left until Christmas.

Fuck, he hated it. Snow. Christmas. The whole damn season. He dreaded it like a millstone. Every goddamn year.

Breath swirling about his face, Silas trudged toward the center of Wolf Pack Run. Whatever the hell the packmaster was apt to blame him for now, he'd sooner get it over with before he retreated back to his cabin—alone. It was bad enough that over the past several days, the whole of the pack hadn't been able to stop casting wary glances in his direction. But then they'd had to go and summon him, and to the Grey Wolf packmaster's office no less.

Like a rabid dog on a leash.

Silas growled, sifting his way through the snow. This time of year, all decked out for the holidays, the dusted cabins and glittering birch halls of Wolf Pack Run, the Grey Wolves' ranch, looked like a scene from a fucking Hallmark card. Romantic. Cozy. Charming. A promise of warm hearths and even warmer company mixed with holiday cheer.

But never for him.

Outside the main compound, several females huddled near the cabin entry. At the sight of him, their group erupted in a hiss of whispers before they eased inward, shrinking closer to one another. To protect themselves. From him. Their former enemy turned packmate. A walking nightmare in cowboy boots.

Oh, for fuck's sake.

"What are you looking at?" he snarled, letting his frustration loose.

Abruptly, the females scattered, letting out several little *eeps* as they retreated in different directions. At least one or two had the courtesy to mutter some vague excuse, before shifting into their wolf forms and disappearing into the ranch's ether. A feat made easier by the endless flurry of snowfall.

Silas grumbled. Good fucking riddance.

"Do you have to antagonize them like that?" The voice was tinged with amusement.

Silas turned to find Wes Calhoun, his former packmaster turned Grey Wolf second-in-command, leaning against the great hall's doorway. Against the backdrop of ice and snow, the smirk which pulled the other wolf's lips coupled with the pale hue of his blond hair made him look every bit the villain he'd once been.

Silas scowled, unable to hide his annoyance. It didn't matter. The Grey Wolves didn't trust him as far as they could throw him. It'd been over a month since Silas had sworn fealty to their pack, longer since he'd been brought here against his will, forced to assimilate, but still, they didn't consider him one of their own.

He was their boogeyman. The Krampus to their Santa.

Why change course now?

"Once a Wild Eight, always a Wild Eight," Silas grumbled. "Except for you."

Wes frowned, before he nodded to where the females had gone. "They'll come around."

"Not for me." Silas' scowl deepened. "*You* came willingly."

Wes shrugged. "Circumstances change, brother. Sometimes you have to change with them."

"Do you tell yourself that or do you really believe it?" Silas shot back, his words a thinly veiled growl. He pegged his former packmaster with a hardened stare. Moving to step around the other wolf, he tried to make his way into the hall, but Wes placed a rough hand on his shoulder.

"Is that what you wanted? To stay with the Wild Eight?" Wes' words stopped him short, wrapping around him like a dark promise of what'd once been.

Silas snarled, teeth bared. Fuck if he knew what he wanted. Then or now.

His future felt as cloudy as the endless gray stretch of Montana sky.

Still, he felt himself hesitate.

"It was better than here," he answered finally. "Anything's better than here."

"You don't really mean that." Wes squeezed his shoulder. "Give it time."

Silas shook his head, pulling from Wes' hold. Time only deepened wounds. Never healed them. He was reminded of that harsh truth every Christmas. "Time is all I have, *packmaster*," he hissed. "I'd think you of all wolves would understand that."

Silas pushed past the other wolf, prowling into the warmth of the main hall as he headed toward his new leader's office. The Grey Wolves would never trust him. Not in the way they trusted

Wes. The ghosts of his past would always haunt him. Every Christmas.

And the Grey Wolves would never allow him to forget it.

~

WHEN SILAS ENTERED the packmaster's office, Maverick Grey sat at his behemoth of a desk, wearing a pair of glasses that should have belonged to a wolf twice his age. In spite of the hair tied at the nape of his neck and the black tattoos poking out from beneath his long-sleeved flannel, from the way the Grey Wolf packmaster poured over the ranch's ledgers, he looked like Ebenezer Scrooge himself. Though Silas was no warm-hearted Bob Cratchit.

At his entrance, the packmaster glanced up, squinting at him slightly through the gleam of the gold lenses before he removed the half-moon spectacles. He cast them onto the desk beside his old, battered Stetson, before lifting a brow expectantly. In the glow of the firelight, the gesture highlighted the notched scar there, a holdover from an old knife wound by an enemy rogue wolf, or so Silas had been told.

Among their kind, too often legend held truth.

"I can see better in wolf form," Maverick mumbled, his deep voice filling the room. He gestured to the now-folded glasses.

Silas fought not to roll his eyes. Of course he could. By his birth right Maverick-fucking-Grey had been gifted every bloody power a wolf could possess. Silas wasn't bitter about it. Really.

"Sit." Maverick nodded toward a high-backed chair, not hesitating to dole out commands, before he closed the ledger he'd been reading.

Silas dropped into one of the armchairs, taking in the space he'd occupied only a handful of times before as he waited for the packmaster to finally lay into him. Ever since he'd arrived at

Wolf Pack Run he'd been blamed for everything from bad crops to dead animals to a particularly bad bout of fleas that'd been passed around several of the packmembers while in wolf form back near the end of summer. But whatever it was this time, he was prepared for it.

The interior of the office was cozy, warm. Full of dark wood shelves and large-bound tomes which detailed the Grey Wolves' long history. Few who took it at face value would recognize it as the helm of their security room, the central command for all the pack's tactical plans. But whoever was in charge of decorating at Wolf Pack Run had taken care to ensure that, lining the bookcases with boughs of holly and even going so far as to add a small, pine tree behind the packmaster's desk. The fresh scent of it permeated the room, its crimson and gold ornaments glittering in the warm glow of the fireside.

Maverick leaned onto his desk, watching Silas with rapt attention. "I have a favor to ask."

"A favor? Or an order?" Silas didn't bother to hide his annoyance. No point in beating around the bush. "Or is there something else you plan to blame me for?"

The packmaster leaned back in his executive seat, examining Silas like he was some frustrating puzzle none of the pack had managed to solve. "Would you prefer an order, warrior?"

"Orders are all you give. Orders and blame," Silas answered.

Maverick pawed a large hand through the scruff of his beard, before he let out a short huff. "I won't sugarcoat it then." He ran his tongue over the pointed canines of his teeth. "I need you to go to Missoula tonight."

"Fuck no," Silas snarled. He didn't move from his chair. There were few things he wouldn't do, but *this* was one of them.

"It's an order, warrior."

Silas froze, his hands gripping the chair arms, shoulders tight. The choice wasn't his to make. For a moment, he stared at the rough patches on the palm of his hand, the tips of his fingers, more prevalent now from all the ranch work, before slowly clenching his hand into a fist. "No," he said again. "No. I won't do it. You know the ghosts that wait for me there, especially this time of year."

"It's not up for discussion." Maverick's eyes flashed to his wolf. "The vampires have been more active than ever. You know this season's rules. No one leaves the ranch unless it's in pairs, and I need someone to escort the pack mechanic up to the old subpack ranch. A part on one of the snowplows is broken and unless we want the entire compound iced over, you'll go to Missoula to retrieve the part."

Silas' lip curled. "You're doing this to torture me. Put me through my paces." Maverick scowled in return. "If I wanted to torture you, I could without consequence. We both know that." Maverick's gaze met his and stayed there. "Should anything happen, no one will fight the vampires harder than you."

Silas didn't doubt it, and yet...

He didn't know which was worse: the shock of fury he felt at the prospect of Maverick toying with him or the pity which now softened the packmaster's features. Silas scowled again.

The pity. Definitely the pity.

"I understand it won't be easy for you, but I won't trust anyone else with it."

Silas scoffed, starting to rise from his chair. "You don't trust me either."

"That's the whole goddamn point," Maverick growled, baring his teeth in return. "Sit down, warrior." He nodded to the armchair again.

Silas felt himself hesitate, but reluctantly, he did, though fuck if he knew why.

Maybe to prove he wasn't the enemy he'd once been.

Maverick watched him for a long beat, eyeing him like he

couldn't get a read on him. "If you expect to be a part of this pack, you're going to learn that trust isn't given. It's earned." Maverick met his gaze. "And this is your chance to earn mine."

Silas shook his head again. "Wes once warned me you'd do this. Said you'd test me."

"And what else did my second say?" Maverick frowned.

"That if I didn't follow through, it'd be my life."

For a moment, Maverick didn't deign to answer, until finally he said, "I'm *offering* you a life, Silas. A different one than you have now. A better one. A chance for you to be a part of this pack." Maverick cleared his throat. "Take it or leave it."

Silas blew out a long breath before raking his hand over his beard. What was a few hours? A day spent haunted by his past? Would there even be a difference?

He already lived side by side with his ghosts. What was one day more?

"Fuck." His jaw clenched. "When do we leave?"

"Tonight." Maverick reached inside his desk drawer. "It shouldn't take more than a few hours. The pack leaves for our yearly shift-and-run to Bozeman first thing in the morning. You'll need to be back by then or the whole pack won't be together on Christmas."

Silas lifted a brow.

"It's tradition," Maverick said.

Tradition. Christmas. Of course. All his misery linked back to this godforsaken holiday.

"So that's it then? Follow the pack's mechanic to Missoula and play bodyguard?"

"And then you'll have *started* to earn my trust, and the pack's too." Maverick tossed him the keys to one of the pack's many trucks. "And Silas," Maverick gave him a pointed look. "I expect you to take good care of her."

Her?

Silas was about to ask which *her* Maverick meant, before the door to the packmaster's office flew open, bringing with it a gust of cold wind, and from the way his wolf suddenly stirred to attention...

No. Fuck no. Absolutely not.

Anyone but her.

Immediately, a flash of fiery red hair caught his attention, and then as if a ray of sunshine and warmth had whipped through him, the scent of sugar cookies hit his nose like a force. Like someone had dangled a whole damn tray beneath his wolf muzzle until all that he smelled, all that he tasted was vanilla, sugar, and the smallest hint of peppermint.

Enough to make him salivate.

Silas pressed his lips into a hard line, feeling his jaw grind stone, even as his cock gave an eager jerk. Suddenly, the words "take good care of her" made more sense.

Because Cheyenne Morgan, Grey Wolf—and apparently the pack's *only* mechanic—was not for him. She was one the pack's most beloved females. To appearances, a tender-hearted she-wolf, adored by all and coveted by even more. Gorgeous. Sweet. Brilliantly smart. A beautifully scattered, head-in-the-clouds dreamer, if he were the kind of wolf who bought into that whole adorably naïve bit. Even now, as she strolled into the room, she didn't seem to be paying attention to what was two feet in front of her, because why bother to look where she was going when the whole of the pack was always there to catch her?

It *should* have made him sick.

No one was that nice, that kind. Not unless they wanted something.

But what *he* thought didn't matter.

Because the whole pack believed it.

And if the fact she was the pack's smiling ray of red-headed sunshine wasn't enough to keep him away, the unfortunate truth that she'd once saved his life would have been. No one did anyone any favors. Especially him. Not without a price.

And that didn't sit well with him.

Because he wanted her, badly, and he hated it. Almost as much as he didn't trust her.

And it was at that moment, thanks to her daydreaming, that she literally fell into his lap.

Or sat there, by accident, as it were.

Fuck.

2

From the moment Cheyenne entered Maverick's office, she knew something was different. She was hyperaware of that kind of thing. Light, sound, textures. Sensory details. The Christmas decorations, she'd expected, of course. They were there every year. Routine. Dependable. But what caught her attention was that her armchair had been moved further to the right, away from the fireplace, to where she could no longer see the empty cushion that waited there, and now, instead of the soft creak of old cushions as she flopped down, a harsh, grumbling growl rumbled against her ear.

A shiver shot down her spine.

Oh no.

Cheyenne's eyes went wide.

She was sitting on someone.

Touching someone, and she hadn't had time to prepare.

She cringed. This was bad. So so bad. Like when she was five and her mother had forced her to sit on Santa's lap at that horrible human mall for a picture bad. As she turned, she didn't need to see who she'd sat on to know exactly who she'd find there. Now that she was aware of him, she could tell by his smell, the feel, the sheer solid size of where he was pressed against her. She'd memorized all the details. Intimately.

Cheyenne's breath caught as her eyes locked with Silas'. "You're not Santa."

Silas growled, teeth bared. "No."

"You're in my seat." She looked toward him again, before quickly glancing away. Eye contact wasn't her forte. It always felt like she was staring someone down, instead of being polite like the other packmembers would say.

And *this* someone was clearly not pleased with her.

She could tell that much.

"*Your* seat?" Silas lifted a brow. His hands clenched the edge of the old armchair, so hard his knuckles had turned white, but she couldn't tell whether he was angry or . . . she didn't know.

He always seemed angry. Grumpy. To her at least.

"Yes, *my* seat." She gestured to his lap. "I always sit here." She glanced to where Maverick sat at his desk and smiled. "The packmaster even made one of the elite warriors move when I was late for a meeting once."

It'd been a kind gesture. It'd made her feel understood. Seen. Autism and all.

Silas frowned, seemingly unconcerned with the chair's ownership. "And the fact that I'm currently sitting here doesn't matter to you?"

"No." She shook her head. "Except that I'd like you to move please."

Which wasn't *entirely* true, since it was *him* she was sitting on, but it would have been if it were anyone else. In truth, the longer she sat there with him, the more she got used to the idea, which was sometimes how things worked for her. She needed time to acclimate, to process, otherwise she got overstimulated.

She waited a beat, expecting him to slide out from beneath

her, but to her surprise, he didn't. "You're not going to move?" She blinked at him. "I asked nicely."

Silas' dark eyes turned toward hers. This close, they were a warm, honey-brown that didn't really fit the harsh lines of his face. The Adam's Apple on his throat gave a sharp jerk.

"Christ," he grumbled.

The tattoo on his temple twitched.

Abruptly, the packmaster cleared his throat.

Cheyenne glanced between the two men.

Was she missing something?

The packmaster lifted his fist to his lips and coughed, like maybe he was trying to smother a smirk? But she didn't understand why.

There was nothing funny about Silas sitting in her chair.

"I have a meeting," Maverick said finally, clearing his throat. "Cheyenne, make sure you're back in time." He hesitated. "You're certain you're ready this year?"

"I'm ready." She nodded in agreement. Right. The shift-and-run. Their Missoula trip. Maverick had given her a heads up to help her prepare yesterday. She couldn't wait to get her hands on that plow part. There was nothing she loved more. Tinkering. Toying with gears. For hours. Until her nails filled with grease. It was one of the few textures she could actually stand. But they'd needed to be careful about their timing. Regimented. She needed to be back home by morning at all costs, or else she'd miss out on her last Christmas with the pack.

The holidays didn't wait, and neither did the military, especially not MAC-V-Alpha. The clandestine shifter-only unit was known for being unforgiving, to say the least, and this holiday would be her last with the pack for a while, so she wanted it to be perfect.

Which for her meant the same. Routine.

Exactly how she'd planned it.

Maverick glanced between them again, and this time, he didn't hide his grin. "Lock the door on your way out."

Cheyenne watched Silas glare at the packmaster.

A few seconds later, the door to the office closed again, leaving them alone. The fireplace beside them crackled. She wiggled a little, bringing herself closer to its warmth, like the chair *should* have been. In the pack's cells, the first time they'd met it'd been cold. Still below freezing. She'd let him out then, even though she hadn't been supposed to. But two months earlier when the pack had accused him of being out for the packmaster's life, he'd sworn he wasn't guilty, and she'd believed him—and she'd been right.

Her mother always said she was a good judge of character.

Even if reading emotion was a bit more ... difficult.

She glanced toward him. "You're really not going to move?"

"No." He grumbled.

"Why?"

"I'm—" He nearly growled again. "—comfortable."

He didn't *sound* comfortable. "You're comfortable in *my* chair?"

She should have wanted him to move, but for some reason, she didn't. But everything was different with him, wasn't it? Not routine. That's what made him so confusing.

He lifted a brow again. "How can you claim a seat you're not even sitting in?"

"I *am* sitting in it." She shrugged. "Or on you, I guess?"

He swore under his breath. "This is ridiculous."

"I agree. This chair has always been mine."

"And does it feel like yours right *now*, Cheyenne?"

She blinked, hesitated, as she stopped to think.

"No," she admitted. "No, it feels like ... like ... like maybe you think *I* should be the one to move?" She asked it as a question, because honestly, she wasn't certain. But what *was* clear to her was that she was fumbling this situation. Miserably.

Silas' lips drew tight. "Ya' think?" His eyes darted to his lap, where she was sitting again.

Now that he mentioned it, there was something hard and rigid pushing against her backside that felt like...

Oh. *Oh.* Her cheeks flushed, mortification coursing through her.

She nodded. Right. Not *officially* her chair, so...

She scrambled from his lap, a blush turning her whole face crimson as she hurriedly placed herself on the other side of the room. Closer to the fireplace, where her chair *should* have been. Suddenly, the Christmas decorations on the mantel there and everything about this situation felt overwhelming. Usually, she liked the decorations, exactly because she could count on them. They were one of her many routines. There first thing come December 1st and then, gone come January like clockwork. But there was nothing routine about this moment.

She glanced toward him again.

Silas was still watching her, eyes narrowed like a hawk. From how his legs were sprawled, claiming space, he looked like a villainous king on his throne. The tilt of his Stetson cast the dark hollows of his face in shadow, obscuring the view so she couldn't read the small cursive script tattooed there and a light layer of brown hair covered his chin like five o'clock shadow grown a bit too long.

Normally, she hated facial hair. The texture. The feel of it. But on him, she actually sort- of liked it. But it was the *way* he was watching her which caused her to still.

It wasn't as if she'd never been with a man and yet...

He was watching her in that way. Like they were alone. Like *that* was about to happen. Though they'd never done anything close to that. Not yet.

His eyes flashed to his wolf, those golden irises tracking her every move.

She willed hers to do the same, to mask, to mimic his frustration. "What's the problem now?" she snapped.

"What's your end-game?" he growled.

End-game? Cheyenne quirked her head in confusion.

Without warning, Silas stood from the chair, rising to his full height before he prowled toward her. Lord, he was large. Dwarfing the small space between them in that same way Maverick and the other elite warriors did. Except different. Because she was more aware of it somehow. With him, that was always the case.

She'd always been on the small side. Born a bit premature and the runt of the litter. But now she felt downright diminutive—fragile. Like he was a predator, and she was his prey. Which was silly because he wasn't her enemy. Not anymore.

Grumpy and tattooed or not.

"Do you really think you can keep this up the whole trip?" He leaned an arm on the mantel over her head. Like he was pinning her between him and the fireside. "I'll admit, you're cute. But you really think I'll buy into this whole adorable act like your packmates do?" His lip curled with a barely held in snarl. "Cut the bullshit."

Cheyenne didn't know what confused her more. His question or that he'd called her cute. Her stomach twisted a little. "I don't know what you're talking about."

He rounded on her then, dark eyes flashing.

This time, she didn't struggle to read the emotion there.

"You know *exactly* what I'm talking about," he grumbled. "No Grey Wolf in their right mind would have let me out of those cells." He leaned in closer, close enough she could feel the warmth of his breath on her face. Smell him there.

Spearmint toothpaste. A hint of aftershave, and . . .

Something inexplicably male. *Him*. His wolf. His skin.

A chill went down her spine, despite the warmth of the fireside licking at her back.

"Why'd you do it?" he drew nearly nose to nose with her. "Why let me out?"

She stared up at him. "You said you weren't guilty."

His brow furrowed. "And you *believed* me?" he asked like even *he* didn't believe it.

"Yes," she breathed. Hadn't he wanted her to? She didn't know why she was suddenly having a hard time drawing air into her lungs, but she was.

Silas watched her for a long beat, until this time, his eyes fell to her lips.

The little gasp which escaped her was unintended.

He'd kissed her there. Once. A few weeks after she'd saved him. Though she'd been the one to initiate, he'd stolen that kiss from her the moment she'd met his lips. Like a plunderer. A marauder. He'd taken it from her, and it'd become his. Then and now. It'd been a mistake.

She still regretted it.

A dark unamused chuckle tore from his lips as he cast her an almost sinister grin. "Either you're a damn good liar or you're a fool." He shook his head. "I'm not sure which is worse."

Cheyenne frowned. She'd defied the packmaster's orders when she'd let him out then, taken him at his word. She'd even been wounded by their *real* enemy as a result. Sometimes, the scar where the knife had entered her side still ached. Yet she wasn't naïve. Especially not enough to think she and a wolf like Silas would ever be friends.

But she believed in justice. Fairness. In a pack as large as the Grey Wolves, too many times she'd been treated as less than, sometimes downright cruel, because she was different. Not every one of her packmates were kind. But she'd helped him because it'd been the right thing to do. She knew what it was to feel like an outsider because as much as her packmates loved her, she was one, too. None of them really understood her.

Not firsthand.

"Well, I guess I'm a fool then," she said. "Maybe I'm not in my *right mind*." She threw his words back at him. "Whatever that even means." Neurotypical wasn't the norm. The default setting. Not for everyone. She glared at him, willing him to understand that for her normal meant something different. But from the menacing look on his face, he didn't.

She couldn't help but feel a bit of disappointment at that.

She tore her gaze away from him. She was used to the growling, the grumbling, all the things to push other people away. Some of the other alpha wolves did it too, but she didn't much care for it. It stung all the same.

As if he were satisfied, he pushed away from the mantel, crossing the room to leave as he adjusted his Stetson. To think she was going to have to spend the next several hours stuck in the small cab of the pack's truck with him. It wasn't fair.

He'd almost reached the door by the time she'd mustered up the courage to say, "But I was right though, wasn't I?"

Silas froze, taut shoulders writhing with thinly leashed control.

"My trust wasn't misplaced," she said.

Slowly, he turned toward her, sharp eyes glaring, and for a second, she almost got the distinct impression that he *wanted* to scare her. For her to distrust him.

Which only made her feel more confused.

But still, she didn't back down.

"I suppose you'd say I just got lucky, right?" She shrugged. "Unless you think there's some reason I shouldn't have believed you in the first place?"

Silas growled. "Is that a threat?"

Cheyenne shook her head. "No. If I needed to threaten you, I would have just left you in that cell." She marched over to him, grabbing the truck keys which dangled in his hand. To her surprise, he let her. She drew close, entering his personal space in the same way he had hers. She didn't need to be taller than him to intimidate. "I don't need you to come to Missoula with me. Contrary to popular belief, I can handle myself just fine on my own." She turned to lead the way out of Maverick's office.

But the hard thump of Silas' hand barred the door.

"I can't let you do that." Silas stood over her again. "Packmaster's orders."

She lifted a brow. "I thought you didn't care about Maverick's orders?"

He didn't answer for a long moment.

Cheyenne eyed him suspiciously. "What's this trip mean to you?"

For a moment, Silas just stared at her. If his jaw clenched any tighter, his teeth might turn to dust. Along with that tongue that'd once parted the seam of her lips, too.

She tried hard not to think about that.

"It's a trust test," he grumbled.

"A trust test?" She blinked. "And you *want* to pass?"

He didn't answer again, but the way his upper lip curled said enough.

She may not have been good at reading emotional cues, but Silas was anything but subtle.

"So you accuse the first packmember who trusts you of being a fool?" She gaped at him. What sort of strategy was that? "That doesn't make any sense." She threw up her hands in exasperation. This whole situation was exhausting. "I have to gather my tools. I'll meet you at the truck in an hour. Don't be late." She beat him to the door, stepping out into the hall before he made it there first. "Unless you have something better to do than *babysit* me." She felt more than a little resentful about that, even though it hadn't been his decision.

She cast him a grin, before abruptly slamming the door in his face. But the surprise in his expression was worth it. She may not have understood him. Or why when she'd kissed him, he'd stolen her kiss, only to then push her away. But at least, she'd figured out a dramatic exit.

3

An hour later, Silas waited by the old ranch truck, feeling—not for the first time—like *he* was the goddamn fool. He leaned against the old truck's hood, the weight of his muscled frame causing it to let out a rusted groan. The ancient beater of a vehicle Maverick claimed as his own had seen better days, but at least the snow had slowed. For now.

Silas shoved his hands into the pockets of his leather, a poor attempt to stave off the cold.

Across the pasture, Cheyenne bounced toward him, a far too cheery spring in her step. She'd already loaded half a dozen tool kits into the truck bed, insisting that she might need one of them in case whatever part she was trying to retrieve gave her a hard time. She'd nestled them all together in a corner, securing them with a bungee cord like they were expensive, high-end luggage, but Silas didn't have it in him to protest.

He was still reeling from what she'd said in the packmaster's office.

"What's this trip mean to you?"

That gut-wrenching question tore through him.

He wasn't certain he knew the answer to that.

Or if he even wanted to.

He watched her as she approached from a distance, clutching yet another massive toolkit to her chest. He'd offered to carry one, but she seemed almost...protective of them. She caught sight of him standing there then, smiling in that sunshiny way of hers. All bright eyes and happy grins, any sign of their bickering forgotten.

Like she hadn't once kissed him out of fucking nowhere as he'd sat by her hospital bedside, destroying him from the outside in. She'd been the only one who'd believed him then, in his innocence and it'd only gotten her hurt, worse. But she seemed to have forgiven him. Still, the list went on. Like he hadn't reveled in the taste of her mouth, only to push her away. Like he *hadn't* accused her of being deceitful less than an hour ago. Like he hadn't been an ass, both then and now. Like everything in Maverick's office was old news. All of it.

Nothing more than dust in the wind.

Fuck, he hated that goddamn Kansas song.

He swore under his breath.

Ever since she'd slammed that door in his face like she'd actually been hurt by what he'd said, he couldn't shake the feeling that maybe he'd been wrong about her.

Maybe she *was* that nice. That sweet and trusting. Lord knew she'd been trusting enough to kiss him, despite what any members of her pack would think. They knew her better than he did after all, and if she really was that sweet, that innocent...

He frowned.

No wonder Maverick had tasked him with guarding her.

She was a walking accident waiting to happen.

Anyone could take advantage of her.

Especially him.

Silas snarled. Trust test indeed.

He tore his gaze away, glancing toward the glittering, snowy hills. Thanks to the stay in the weather, the whole of Wolf Pack Run was alive now, buzzing with movement as the pack played and celebrated the coming holiday. Tomorrow those able-bodied adults who chose to participate would shift into their true forms, staying wolves for several days as they trekked out into the forest all the way to Bozeman to unite with their sister subpack. Meanwhile, the elders and others who chose to stay behind would care for the pups and children. Only for all of them to gather back home at Wolf Pack Run again.

The tradition was nothing more than a long romp through the snow-covered forest, like the wolves they truly were, except that it ended in all of them together. As one. On Christmas.

Silas scowled. He couldn't say he was looking forward to it.

He glanced back toward Cheyenne again to find her stalled a few meters away with a handful of Grey Wolf males around her. One of them was standing in her path, talking to her with a not-so-subtle grin on his face. Some asshole in a plaid flannel and beanie who looked like he'd stolen his clothes from a hipster rather than a cowboy, though she didn't seem to mind from the way she smiled back.

She was always smiling. At everyone.

It shouldn't have bothered him. He knew how to the whole of the pack felt about her and yet... Inside, his wolf stirred.

He wanted those smiles to be for him and him alone.

And wasn't that all kinds of fucked.

He frowned.

She's not for you.

Silas' gaze darted back toward the group. Asshole was stepping toward her now, trying to take the tools from her to help, but something about Cheyenne's smile stiffened. Silas felt himself tense. She wasn't pleased he was trying to help her.

She was smiling because she was *nervous*.

Before Silas knew what he was doing, he was half-way across the snow-covered pasture, tearing through the snowdrift toward them. He didn't stop until he'd reached Cheyenne's side.

"I . . . I really *really* don't like anyone touching my tools." She laughed. Her voice was still happy, chipper, but there was a worried edge to it that made the cheer less-than-sincere. Fearful.

Anyone would have been blind not to see it.

"I'm just trying to help you, Cheyenne. Why do you have to freak out about everything?" Asshole moved to take the tools again.

As he reached for her, Cheyenne recoiled. Like her packmates' touch wasn't simply unwelcome—though that would have been enough—but like the thought of it genuinely filled her with terror.

Silas didn't think.

He shoved his way between her and her packmate, shielding her behind him. "Get in the truck, Cheyenne," he heard himself saying.

She let out a surprised little sputter. "W-what?"

"Fuck off, Silas. I was just trying to help her."

Silas growled, low and feral. But his eyes didn't leave Cheyenne's. He wasn't ready to deal with the pushy fucker. Not just yet.

"I said get in the truck," he told her again. His eyes flashed to his wolf in warning.

This time, she didn't question him. She did as she was told, trusting him implicitly. Though fuck if he deserved it. Yet.

She stepped around him, scurrying to place her tools into the truck bed with the other kits. Silas waited until she was safely sealed inside the cab before he turned toward her packmate again. *His* packmate.

He still couldn't bring himself to think of them like that.

Asshole was glaring at him now, scowling like he was

looking for a fight. From his smell, he'd already started the Christmas festivities and he was several whiskey and eggnogs in.

"I was trying to help her. She doesn't have to be such a bitch about it." Asshole leered.

"Don't call her that." Silas snarled. "It's not help if she doesn't fucking want it." He stepped away, prepared to leave it at that, but as he walked back toward the truck, Asshole's grating voice followed him.

"Coward." Asshole chuckled. He and his friends laughed. "You Wild Eight bastards always were too scared for your own good."

Silas stilled.

Once a Wild Eight, always a Wild Eight.

He'd said it to Wes only because he'd already heard it so many times before, but hearing it now when he was trying to protect Cheyenne, and from her own packmate, was different.

It was a reminder of everything he'd never have.

Silas swallowed, holding down a growl. Let this idiot call him a coward, worse. All while he hid behind a pack that promised to keep him safe. The Grey Wolves were the leaders of the Seven Range Pact, the rulers of the Montana mountains their kind called home. They could do whatever the hell they liked, and every surrounding shifter pack would follow, support them.

The Wild Eight had never had that privilege. All over a difference of opinion.

Pack politics.

Cowards too often held all the power. Used it as a weapon against others.

This bastard had no idea what a *true* coward was.

Silas refused to take the bait, continuing toward the truck. The last thing he needed was a conflict with some drunken alpha Grey Wolf.

As he reached the cab, Cheyenne poked her head out of the passenger window, searching for him. Just in time to hear Asshole say, "She'd be a better lay, if she wasn't so fucking weird."

Silas stiffened.

Asshole said it like it was some kind of weapon. Something to wound and hurt her. As a descriptor, weird was a pathetic word. Meant for childish school yard bullies. Barely an insult. At least, to him. But as Silas watched Cheyenne visibly cringe, he knew it meant something *different* for her. Something far crueler.

And he didn't think she was weird. He thought she was perfect.

Too good for him.

Too good he hadn't even thought she could be real, at first. But now he regretted that.

She shrunk into the truck cab, that sparkle in her eyes dimming. Silas didn't know what exactly her packmate's cruelty meant to her, but he didn't need to.

He didn't think. He simply moved.

He was gripping the other Grey Wolf alpha by the back of his head before he could blink, holding the other wolf by a fistful of hair. He slammed the asshole's face down onto the edge of the truck bed with a satisfying crunch of broken nose. Blood poured from the wound, drenching the other wolf's flannel shirt.

Asshole howled. "What the fuck?" He pawed at his face.

But Silas wasn't finished yet.

Without warning, he tore his blade from his boot, thankful that the pack hadn't declawed him of *all* his weapons. Yet.

He shoved the tip of his dagger against the bastard's throat, backing him up against the truck until he forced him to expose the skin of his neck. Had they been in wolf form, who the dominant wolf was couldn't have been any clearer.

"Yeah, she's different," Silas growled. "But who the fuck isn't?"

What the hell even *was* normal for wolf shifters anyway?

Inches from the other wolf's face, he snarled, teeth bared. "Insult her again and I'll fucking end you. Are we clear?"

Asshole gave a single, curt nod.

Silas released him with a harsh shove—not bothering to see if he landed on the truck bed or in the mixture of dirt and snow.

Without looking back, he climbed into the truck, slamming the door shut behind him and locking the doors. Cheyenne passed him the keys. The truck's old engine roared to life, churning and sputtering as he pressed down the gas pedal. They were nearly at the edge of the Grey Wolves' ranchlands, heading out onto the nearest highway before either one of them spoke again.

"Why'd you do that?" Cheyenne whispered.

She spoke the words so quietly that if it wasn't for the snow dampening the sounds of the winter winds, he wasn't certain he would have heard her.

"Why'd you defend me like that?" she asked again.

"I don't know." He switched on the truck's heater, refusing to take his eyes from the road. A few seconds later, the heater purred, spilling warmth into the cab. Though Silas' blood already felt heated, warm. It did every time he was near her. He gave a rough clear of his throat. "Why'd you believe me?" He dared glance toward her then.

She was watching him with eyes so wide and owlish it was like she'd never seen him before. A man could easily get lost in the amber warmth in them.

He cleared his throat again. "That first night. In the cells, I mean."

"Because it wasn't fair," she whispered. "You were there because of other people's fear. Not your actions."

Silas shook his head, navigating the truck out onto the freshly salted roads. "I didn't ask why you let me out." He gripped the steering wheel tighter. "I asked why you *believed* me?"

"I don't know," she said. "I just did."

Silas nodded. Shifting the old truck's clutch into first gear. He understood the feeling.

And the thought terrified him.

4

Cheyenne loved the feeling of grease on her hands. She laid on her back underneath one of the Missoula subpack's abandoned trucks, working to disconnect the hydraulic plow. Okay, maybe *love* was an exaggeration, but it was one of the few textures she could tolerate.

It was partially why she'd became a mechanic. That and her fascination with anything which had a motor, an engine, gears. Back at Wolf Pack Run, the pack had several larger, more industrial sized machines for when they were snowed in, but this little Husqvarna attachment could reach narrower places, and the one back at the main ranch had puttered out.

She shivered a little, trying to ignore the cold at her back as she worked. At least her true nature was keeping her somewhat warm. Her wolf enjoyed the cold. No way could she do this without gloves and laying in the snow if she'd been human. She'd started off with a pair to cover her hands of course, but once she'd acclimated, she'd quickly abandoned them.

She liked to *feel* the metal in her hands as she tinkered, worked.

"Are you almost done?" Silas grumbled again.

It was maybe the tenth time he'd asked it.

He'd been on edge since the moment they'd arrived, though Cheyenne couldn't say she blamed him. There was something eerie about the now-abandoned ranch, about knowing that the handful of shifters, her subpackmates, who used to live here had lost their lives to their bloodsucking enemies here only a few years before. Not long past Christmas.

As a former Wild Eight, Silas would understand that kind of violence firsthand. The mark it left on the land. It changed a man. Or so she'd been told.

"Almost." Cheyenne grunted as she tried to loosen a particularly icy lug-nut. Her wrench couldn't seem to get a hold on it now that she was in a hurry. She'd spent more time exploring the truck's stalled out engine than she should have before she'd started in on her true task.

"We were supposed to be back on the road before nightfall," Silas reminded her again.

She was far too aware that had been the plan, at least. But when they'd arrived, the truck hadn't been parked in the garage like the pack inventory sheet had said. Like it was supposed to be. It'd taken time to locate it. Time they hadn't had. The deviation in the plan had made her nervous, irritated. Whoever had been up here last to gather supplies or work on the old ranch's restoration clearly hadn't returned it to its rightful spot like they were supposed to. So then the tinkering began as a way to cope. The concentration on work.

As soon as she'd gotten under the truck's hood, she'd taken comfort from being off schedule by doing what she loved. Working with her hands.

She had a hard time pulling herself out when her focus locked in like this.

Time failed to matter. Like it disappeared.

"I'll just be another minute," she said.

Silas growled again, but this time, it sounded harsher. More warning. "Cheyenne."

She let out an annoyed huff, frustration racking through her. She *hated* to be interrupted when she was hyper-focused like this. "I *said* I'll be done in just a—"

A rough calloused hand pressed over her mouth.

Cheyenne stiffened. Froze.

She glanced toward him then. Silas was crouched beside the truck now, his hand pressing over her mouth to quiet her. She had to fight to keep still, not to recoil and he seemed to realize it, that she didn't like to be touched suddenly or without warning, because slowly, he removed his hand from her lips, lifting a single finger to his own to indicate she should be quiet.

Making her realize there was a reason for it.

Careful not to make a sound, she slipped out from underneath the vehicle. The snow had picked up considerably while she worked, coming down so heavy it made it difficult even for her nocturnal eyes to see. Night had already fallen around them. The shadows darkened the abandoned ranch into an endless stretch of starry Montana sky. The snow beneath glittered like it too was made of stardust instead of an infinite number of tiny ice crystals.

It was breathtaking, beautiful really, and yet, something about it felt off, eerie.

Silently, Silas nodded toward the trees, to the darkened snarled branches of the forest. It was a sight her wolf normally would have welcomed, like the trees were calling her home, but right now, it looked a bit sinister with the whole of the ranch abandoned, empty like this. Silas' eyes flashed to the golden glow of his wolf, silently confirming.

There was something out there. In the darkness.

Cheyenne stilled.

Vampires.

She'd thought Maverick had been being overcautious. All things considered. She hadn't actually expected any of their bloodsucking enemies would follow them out here and so near Christmas. A shuddered exhale tore from her lips, causing her breath to swirl around her face like smoke.

Silas shook his head, pressing another finger to his lips to remind her to stay quiet, before abruptly, he shifted into his wolf. His clothes and the pack issued cell phone in his pocket fell to the ground in an abandoned heap as bone, sinew, and limbs twisted. A moment later, he was nudging his cold, damp nose against her hand, her leg, urging her to join him. But she was frozen, immobile.

Nipping at her ankles, he slowly herded her a few steps to the right, rubbing and nudging against her. The fur of his coat brushed against her skin of her human form, making her remember herself, working her through her fear. Long enough to allow her to join him.

She shook her head, focusing enough so that she was on all four paws beside him a moment later. The sensation of shifting back and forth had been one she had to get used to when she'd been a child, first learning to shift, but she'd been doing it so long now that'd it'd become second nature. As much as part of her as her autism.

Different and yet full of its own kinds of beauty, strength.

Silas nipped again at her side, the scruff of her neck until she turned her attention to him. He jumped, spreading out his paws in a wide stance to indicate he was about to run, and she should join him. She didn't think. She just trusted him. She had from the start.

She didn't know why, but she'd known he was good. Noble. Even then.

Silas ran through the snow, leading the way as she followed. Far enough until she felt like all fear of the vampires had been forgotten. On paw like this she felt stronger. Fiercer. Like her teeth and claw would be enough. Even if Silas' failed her. Not that she was certain any vampire would manage to get through him. The Wild Eight may have been their enemies, but they'd been intense fighters. A force to be reckoned with. Even for the Grey Wolf pack.

He led her deeper and deeper into the darkness of the ranch. As if he knew exactly where he was going. Like he had a plan. The snow had picked up so intensely that even in her wolf form, she could hardly see two feet in front of her. But still, Silas kept going, leading the way.

He didn't stop until they reached an abandoned cabin.

One more secluded, away from the rest.

Drawing up on the door, he shifted back into human form, using the whole of his strength to force the door open enough for them to slip through the crack. Snow was already starting to block the underside, but still, he ushered her in. She didn't shift back into her skin again until he'd closed the door and locked it behind them. Giving herself a little shiver from head to toe, she shook the snow from her limbs, trying not to pay attention to the fact that she was naked, and he was too. It was part of pack life. Normal for them and their species, and yet...

In the darkness, alone with him, she felt exposed in a way she shouldn't have.

Cheyenne breathed out a rough breath. Even in the cabin she could see it swirl in the cold. She was even colder now that she was back in human form. "Are you certain there were vampires out there? I didn't see anything."

Though she'd felt them. She just hadn't fully settled into the idea they'd been near danger just yet. Because running with him, being in wolf form as they raced across the mountainside together had felt so freeing, and she hadn't quite figured out her own emotions about that.

"Gut instinct," Silas grumbled. As if that explained everything.

It didn't.

Cheyenne shook her head, barely paying attention to the dark abandoned cabin around them.

Silas tried to flip on one of the light switches but not even a bulb flickered. "Fuck me," he muttered under his breath. "And no phone either. Great. Just great."

Cheyenne couldn't begin to understand what was remotely great about that. Sarcasm was confusing. "We can't stay here long. Not if they're out there. We need to grab that part and get back on the road."

Silas shook his head, casting a frustrated glance at her through the dark. All she could see of him right now was a pair of glowing gold eyes and a dark outline of his muscled form. "We're not getting back on the road tonight."

"What?" Inside, Cheyenne reeled. Panicked. Her pulse started to race. "We *have* to. You heard the packmaster. We need to be home by morning for the shift-and-run."

Most of the adults in the pack participated, planned on it. It was part of her routine, seeing them off. Every year. And this year, she'd finally worked up the courage to participate.

"They can wait." Silas' lip curled in distaste. "Maverick would want you to."

Why did he say the packmaster's name like that? So full of resentment? "They're not going to wait. They're going to—"

"—*Your* packmaster tasked me with protecting you. Keeping you safe." His dark eyes flashed. "That's what I'm trying to do."

She blinked at him. "He's your packmaster too."

Silas grumbled. "In name only. Even he knows it."

Cheyenne recoiled. "What's *that* supposed to mean? You're a Grey Wolf now."

At her reaction, something inside Silas seemed to snap then, whatever tenuous leash he seemed to have on himself breaking. He rounded on her, drawing close. Close enough she could see the outline of his lips through the darkness. The fullness of them. She could feel him almost pressed against her. His closeness and warmth.

"Even if I wanted to be, your packmates wouldn't let me," he hissed. There seemed to be more meaning in those words than he was letting on, something emotional, but Cheyenne couldn't parse it out right now.

Not when she was faced with all ... this.

The chaotic feeling that roared inside her at the sudden change of plans.

The glare of the moon. The unfamiliar creak of the floorboards. It was all too much.

She was two tiny steps away from overstimulation, teetering on the edge unless she managed to get a hold of it. She tried to force herself to breathe, to take slow breaths in and out through her nose.

"That's not true," she said. "They've already accepted you. You've already sworn fealty to the pack." She'd seen the ceremony with her own two eyes, witnessed it.

"Only for them to throw me in the cells a few days later because they suspected I was out to kill your leader." Silas snarled. "Tell me they would have done that to a *true* packmember."

Now that he pointed out, she could see the nuance there, even if she struggled to grasp it, understand. But what he failed to notice is that the pack had allowed him to become one of them in the first place. They wouldn't have done that if they hadn't meant it. Would they?

"You can't blame them for making a mistake," she said.

Slowly, he lifted a hand, hesitated, until she nodded her approval. Gently, he brushed it over her cheek. "They blame me. For all their troubles. You've seen it. You said it was unfair."

She had, yet...

"I didn't mean you shouldn't forgive them." Her hands were jittering at her side, dangerously close to flapping now. Maybe she should let them to calm herself, but she didn't want him to see it. She didn't want him thinking she was strange. Not him. Not just yet.

"How can you expect to be one of us when you keep pushing everyone away?" she snapped. The words were out before she could draw them back in. Blunt and brutally honest.

Silas snarled. Dropped his hand. "What the fuck does that mean?"

"*That*," she said, pointing at him. The harshness in his face. "*That's* what I mean. When you do *that*. You can't expect anyone to like you, to want to be near you when you're snarling at them all the time. It makes people think you're grumpy and mean, and you're not. Not really," she breathed.

Silas froze. Even in the dark, his whole body seemed to stiffen, recoil. "And how would you know that?" The words dripped with venom. Pain.

"I just ... do okay?" She couldn't explain it. "I've seen it in you from the start." She shrugged, fighting to keep her hands at her side. "You try to push people away, but it's only because you're scared, hurt. Like a wounded animal." She shrugged. "My mom always said I was a good judge of character," she said, repeating the words. Masking. Mimicking.

In an attempt to cope.

"Bully for you." Silas snarled, stepping away from her.

Bully for—?

Cheyenne watched him prowl through the cabin's darkness. "What does that even mean?"

"You tell me."

She lost it then. All sense of control. "You're not making any sense," she keened. She couldn't keep her hands at her side any longer. "I'm ready to go home now. Let's get the part and go." She made to move toward the door.

But Silas turned toward her, backlit by the moonlight from where he'd glanced out the window. A gruff curse came from his lips. "We can't."

"Why not?" she nearly whimpered, rocking. Forget the part. They could do without it. But she *had* to be back home to Wolf Pack Run in time. She *had* to be. Or else she'd miss out on her last Christmas with the pack. Break her routine. Her plans.

The thought alone made her hands start to shake even harder.

"We're here for the night," Silas said, as if it'd already been decided.

The finality of those words shook her.

"The vampires are going to be lurking about that long?" She felt herself starting to hyperventilate.

"No, but even if they were, we can't leave." Silas' words were a thinly veiled growl.

"Why not?" They were half words, half shriek. She was full on stimming now. Unable to stop herself. But in the darkness, Silas seemed unaware.

"Because," he snarled, trying the door and cursing again. "We're snowed in for fuck's sake."

5

Only in Montana could snow plummet to the ground that goddamn fast. It'd been coming down like there was no tomorrow when they were running, so thick he could hardly see. It'd already been starting to pile up then. But instinct and memory had fueled him, driving him to the one place he'd known how to get to even with his eyes closed. All to keep them safe.

Even if it tore him to shreds.

Everything was difficult about being here, even in the dark. The dust all around them. The intact furniture that indicated someone else had moved in long ago. Taken over in the years he'd left since. The lack of family portraits that used to hang all over this place, the ones he was accustomed to seeing on the walls, here and in his memories, were long since gone. Lost to the years. Every bit of it cut him deep enough it felt like he wouldn't be whole again.

But he couldn't think of that right now. Not when Cheyenne was standing in front of him, clearly and desperately needing him.

No. Not him. Just someone. Anyone.

He just happened to be the needy bastard assigned to protecting her.

"Cheyenne," he said her name, low and slow, drawled it like he would to a startled horse.

She was flapping her hands all over the place, pacing back and forth as she made a repeated humming noise. Like she was having some kind of panic attack or something.

"Cheyenne," he said her name, again, trying to draw her attention.

When she didn't answer him immediately, he acted on pure instinct, doing what he hoped someone would do for him had he ever felt the same. He approached her slowly, gently touching her arm. She jumped suddenly, like she might shy away. But he didn't let her.

"Let me hold you," he said.

She gave him a small, barely-there nod. He wrapped his arms around her in seconds. Brought her firmly to his chest. If he could just hold all the pieces of her together, she might not break. It took a moment, but she settled into his arms, against the heavy weight of him over her. She shivered a little, like everything inside her was poised to vibrate, but he just held on tighter. Fuck, if he didn't understand why she needed it.

But he did too.

Christ. He'd known coming here was a mistake.

Foolish even.

"It's all right, baby. Just breathe." Tentatively, he reached up and stroked a hand through her fiery hair. The strands fell like silk between his fingers. Softer than he'd imagined. Or remembered, from the last time he'd tangled his hands there. When she'd kissed him before, he hadn't been able to help himself. But he was glad for that now. For stopping. Now that he knew she was real, really as sweet as she seemed, he couldn't allow himself to take advantage.

A wolf like him wasn't for her.

"I promise I'll try and get you back in time." He said it because he couldn't think of anything else, but the moment the words passed his lips, the tension in her lessened.

Significantly.

"Is that what was worrying you?"

She nodded. Still jittery.

Silas couldn't help it, but he chuckled to himself. "Damn you're really a sucker for tradition."

"Routines," she breathed against his shoulder. "I like routines."

He nodded. He could remember that.

Slowly, as the tension in her body lessened, the length of the hug, the intensity of how tight he was holding onto her became . . . awkward, filled with tension. Silas gave a rough clear of his throat, before he stepped back. Any longer holding her and it was going to turned heated, fast.

"Thanks," she whispered, as he stepped away from her.

He didn't like it when she thanked him. Not for something like that. Not for something any half-decent person would do. Which was the perfect way to describe him, half-decent. Both considering they were nude and the fact that his past was still something he was trying to reconcile. He supposed there was no better place than here to make sense of it.

Though he couldn't allow himself to think about that just yet.

"There's likely a bed or a couch since there's still furniture in here," he grumbled. "I doubt they'll send anyone out to look for us until the storm clears. I'll find some blankets."

Cheyenne's stomach growled.

"Are you hungry?"

She nodded.

"There might be a can of something left over in the pantry or cabinet from when . . ." He heard himself hesitate. "From whoever the fuck last lived here," he mumbled.

He didn't like to think about that. The time this place had spent abandoned. Or worse, the time it'd been occupied in the years since by someone who wasn't him, only to return to being abandoned again. Like it was cursed. Him, this place, these hills.

Though he knew the only true curse was the choices he'd made. He'd done this.

And those bloodsucking fuckers. Wherever they were.

He hated them. For everything they'd taken from him. Now and then.

Silas shook his head, moving to step toward the pantry.

"No thanks," Cheyenne said. "I-I can't stand the texture of canned food."

The texture?

Silas shrugged, convinced it was some bourgeoisie shit that came with being raised a Grey Wolf at Wolf Pack Run, where the pack had anything and everything they wanted at their fingertips. Life in the subpacks was harder. But bearable. Happy even.

Though never as well protected. That dark hole inside him, where his grief lived, filled with resentment. Rage. That was where he lived these days. Because it was familiar. He'd spent so long there, he didn't know how to get out of it again. Didn't even know if he could. She'd been right when she said he pushed others away. But fuck if he knew how to stop himself from doing it. It'd become second nature.

"Right. Texture," he grumbled, as if he had any idea what the hell that meant. "I'll find some blankets." He started to head to where he knew the linen closet used to be, but felt himself hesitate. He paused before he turned back toward her.

The way she looked standing there, naked in the moonlight that streamed through the window was . . . Well, he didn't know. He wasn't the sort of man to say something took his breath away.

But she did then. Even as he felt guilty for it, knowing she was vulnerable after—whatever that was. Now more than ever.

"Are-are you going to be okay while I go do that?" He pawed at the back of his neck sheepishly. Even to his own ears the question sounded strange. Sincere, yet forced. Like he'd been out of practice being nice for too long. Shit.

Maybe she really was right about him.

If Cheyenne noticed the change, she didn't say anything. She wrapped her arms around herself, glancing out into the darkness. The nearly full moon hung in the sky overhead, obscured by the relentless fall of snow.

"Yeah," she whispered, nodding like she was trying to reassure herself. "Yeah, I'll be okay."

Silas nodded, then made his way through the darkened cabin, searching for any sort of linen or sheets. He tried not to catalogue all the changes as he went. All the life that'd clearly happened there. Without him. Without any of the family he'd loved either.

When he finally located an old quilt wedged in the far back of an empty cabinet, he heard Cheyenne's voice call out to him from one of the bedrooms.

"Silas."

He grunted in response.

"There's only one bed in here."

Silas closed his eyes, even as his hands clenched, tightening until he was fisting huge handfuls of the fucking quilt. He couldn't catch a break tonight, could he?

6

Cheyenne had no idea how she was ever going to sleep. Her mind was still reeling from overstimulation. From the change in routine. Her plans. The darkness. Nothing around her felt familiar. It was all too much. She glanced over to where Silas lay, still and solid beside her.

He'd offered to sleep on the floor, curled up in wolf form. But she wasn't about to kick him out of the only bed in this place when him leading her here was the only reason she was still breathing, alive. If the vampires had found her while working on that tractor alone, they wouldn't hesitate. He didn't need to break a nose like he'd done with Cayden, their packmate, in order to protect her. Vigilance. Awareness of surroundings was enough because the vampires hadn't even found them. But they'd gotten close.

Silas' gut instinct seemed honed like a blade.

If how he'd held her when she'd been stimming was any indication.

He'd been a natural, both then and in the pasture, like he'd known exactly how to help her. Even at a time when she hadn't been able to help herself.

"Silas," she whispered over to where he lay beside her.

He didn't answer.

"Silas."

"Mmm." He grunted.

"Are you asleep?"

"Not *now*," he grumbled, his voice graveled, husky.

A rush of heat shot to her core. But she willed herself not to think like that. He'd already shown he wasn't interested. He'd pulled away when they'd last kissed. Though even *she* had to admit that the fact that he'd kissed her back in the first place, not to mention that her sitting on his lap had given him a way-too-impressive erection, was a little bit... contradictory.

But there were more important things to consider in this case.

"Do you think the vampires will find us here?" she whispered, pulling up the covers so that they shrouded her head as she watched him through the darkness. He still hadn't turned to face her. Her eyes traced over the planes of his back, the corded muscle there.

But she couldn't stop thinking about the tracks they'd left in the snow, about whether they'd be covered up by now. Forgotten.

Something about that idea made her a little sad. Disappointed even. Though she knew it was for the best. She didn't want their enemies tracking them, especially this late. When they were snowed in and vulnerable. The darkness around them was all encompassing with no lights for miles. But she didn't want the memory of them erased by the snow.

Silas rolled away from her a little further. "I think the vampires are long gone."

"And you don't think they'll come looking for us again?" Her voice was a whispering hiss against his ear.

"No." Silas groaned, stretched. "Not now that we've made it

difficult for them." He glanced over his shoulder toward her. "And would you stop fucking breathing on me like that? It's . . . tempting." He reached around to the front of his hips, adjusting himself.

A blush filled her cheeks.

"Sorry." She eased back, embarrassed again. She was still mortified over him watching her meltdown earlier and now this. "Sorry. I just-I normally sleep with a weighted blanket, and I'm cold and you're warm, and—"

The growl that escaped him caused her to shiver. "Are you going to come over here, or are you going to keep me awake all night?"

"Both?"

Silas let out a harsh, hiss of a curse.

"I'm sorry." She winced. "Definitely both."

He snarled. "Fuck me. It never turns off does it?"

"What doesn't turn off?"

"You. This. The—" He struggled to find the right word. "The sunshine and roses bit."

"I wasn't sunshine and roses earlier."

He grumbled. "I mean aside from that."

"Aside from that?" She thought for a moment. "No. I'm always this . . . weird." She hated that word, the way it othered her.

"I don't think you're weird, Cheyenne."

Her smile faded a bit. "You'd be the only one."

Silas rolled onto his back, staring up at the ceiling. One large arm perched behind his head. She tried not to stare at the curve of his bicep, the tattoos there. She really did.

"I think you're naive. Innocent. Like your head's stuck in the clouds. Far too sweet. Like you could give me a fuckin' toothache. But not weird."

"Sweet," she repeated it. "I think I can deal with that."

"Are you going to come over here or not?"

"This is strictly platonic," she said. "Necessity."

He cleared his throat. "You feel the need to tell yourself that?"

"No. I-I felt the need to tell you since . . . " She felt herself hesitate. "Since you clearly didn't want me to kiss you that-that time that I did."

~

Silas didn't know what the hell to say to that. She was wrong. So horribly, incredibly wrong. He had no idea how the woman now scooting over into his arms could have thought that he didn't want to kiss her, but somehow, she did. It'd been weeks ago. Back in the pack's hospital wing, when she'd still been healing from her injury. The moment her lips had touched his, he'd nearly ravished her damn mouth. He'd been wild with need. Fucking savage with the taste of her on his tongue. He'd barely been able to pull himself back. Restrain himself.

He was struggling with the same problem right now.

But who could blame him?

This beautiful woman. This tender, kind, curious woman was lying naked in his arms, snuggled against him like she wanted to soak up all of his body heat, curl into him and it was pure unadulterated torture that she wasn't already riding his cock.

Fuck this noise.

Fuck Maverick and the Grey Wolves for tempting him with what he couldn't have.

He eased his hips back, in an attempt to behave, placing some distance between their lower halves and nudging the thin material of the sheet between them, but it was hardly any use. She kept drawing closer, and he kept inching farther in this strange sort of push-and-pull dance. But his bare ass was nearly hanging off the side of the bed now, so there wasn't anywhere left to go, until...

"Silas?" she whispered, drawing closer again.

"Mmm," he grunted. He wasn't certain he could form words right now and still keep himself restrained, not with all the blood in his body rushing straight to his throbbing dick. His balls ached, strained.

"Why do you keep scooting away?"

Goddamn it. He'd been asking himself just that.

He gritted his teeth. "I'm not supposed to want you, Cheyenne."

She frowned. "I don't understand."

Silas growled. Shit. How was he going to explain this and keep himself in check? He blew out a long steadying breath. "Maverick told me to take care of you. Not to touch you. That's the trust test."

"What?" She sat up slightly, anger twisting her face. Enough that the sheet slipped away, exposing one of her breasts.

Silas' cock throbbed. Goddamn it, he was losing this battle and fast.

"Why would he do that?" Cheyenne looked livid.

"Fuck if I know," Silas mumbled under his breath, trying to resist looking at her, and failing. His eyes zeroed in on her perfect pert nipple. He wanted to run his tongue all over it, tease it with his teeth, use his tongue to explore other hidden things. Between her legs namely. His mouth watered. "Probably because I'm not good enough for you," he heard himself saying.

As soon as he admitted it, he wanted to take it back. He was making a mess of this, rambling as he struggled to control himself. Getting dangerously close to the truth. But that's what darkness did, wasn't it? Made it safe for more than bare skin to be exposed.

Silas swallowed.

"Is that why you pulled away when I kissed you?" Cheyenne asked with an annoyed huff, sinking back down into the sheets. Silas growled, low and feral, wanting to wrench the covers off her the moment her gorgeous breasts disappeared from him. He wanted to bury his face there. He didn't even need to breathe. Who needed air when he could have *that*?

"Is that why?" she asked again, drawing his attention. "Because you think you're not a Grey Wolf? Because you think you aren't good enough?"

Silas shook his head. He couldn't do this. Not now. Not when his control was already stretched so thin it was tenuous at best. His wolf stirred beneath his skin, every inch of him aware of how close she was. Naked and open to him. All he had to do was reach out and take her. No one was here to stop him, snatch her back from him, steal her away.

He could fuck her until she was screaming his name, and no one would ever know.

No one but them. He was certain of that.

"I don't deserve you," he said.

But I want to.

He had to bite his own tongue to keep from whispering it.

"I don't know what you mean by that." Cheyenne's brow furrowed. Those full lips pulled into an angry pucker. "Who said you have to be deserving?" He felt her weight on the mattress move beside him. Felt the heat of her. Smelled that warm vanilla scent. "Don't I get a choice?"

There was righteous anger in her question, the kind of rage that was warranted, and Silas didn't know what to do with that. Or himself for that matter. Shielded by the dark and the sheet between them, he took his cock into his own hand, giving the head one hard stroke like that might ease the ache. It didn't. Fuck, it made it worse. So much worse.

His balls tightened.

All he could think about was her touching him like that.

Finally, she let out a long sigh and whispered. "I need you to be direct, please. If you don't want me, just say so, so I can understand that."

Silas should have left it at that. His exit path was right there. All he had to do was take it. Tell her he didn't want her. He should have told her those words exactly and left at that.

But he couldn't. Not when she was practically begging him for it.

He had her in his arms, pulling her flush against him as he used one large hand to part the bare skin of her thighs within seconds. He thrust the thick length of his cock there, rubbing the outside of her perfect slit with it, until the slick heat of her pressed overtop his shaft.

He growled. "How's that for direct?"

Her breath caught, he felt it hitch, but he didn't stop. He wasn't anywhere near finished with her yet. "I'm not very good at being gentle," he purred against her ear. He tugged at the lobe with his teeth, working his way down with tongue and tooth until he was between her bare breasts. He sucked one into his mouth, causing her to arch against him, teasing and kneading and fondling it until he bit down, hard. "But I'll try."

She gasped, keened.

"You okay with that?" he whispered.

She nodded, nuzzling her cheek against him as her lips brushed against his. "I think so," she breathed. "Just don't break me. Please."

Silas grumbled a near chuckle. "I'm not going to do that, sugar. I'm going to put you back together." He kissed her, licking over the seam of her lips, gaining entry before he pulled back enough to whisper against her mouth. "But I *am* going to make you scream."

7

Cheyenne had never experienced so many sensations at once before. Her whole body had come alive. Sure, she'd had sex a handful of times. Different partners even. But never anything like this. No one had ever promised to make her scream. No one had ever made her want to beg, plead for more. So much more it made her feel greedy, hungry with need. Too often sex was like an out of body experience for her. Something she was there for, but never fully present.

But she was present now. Fully with Silas like she was supposed to be. At ease in her own her skin in a way she'd never felt before. And she had no idea what to do about that.

If that was how it was supposed to be.

Silas seized the lead, taking the reins from her with a wild, hungry command and she followed, uncertain what to do except receive, react. His tongue was exploring her mouth now, deepening the kiss until other parts of her started to ache. Her breasts felt heavy, and the heat between her legs grew slick. As if he knew, sensed it, he palmed her breasts, inching his hands lower until his cock wasn't the only thing teasing the outside of her entrance. The rough pad of his thumb circled the sweet bead of her of her clit.

She groaned. How had he found it so quick? He hadn't even seemed to be looking.

Every other man she'd been with had acted like it was some buried, hidden treasure sunk deep into the bottom of the sea. There, but too difficult to find.

But Silas didn't. He knew exactly how to touch her so she keened. In a way that was both too much and not enough. Steady. Rough. Competent.

He was her first she realized. Her first man.

All her previous lovers had been boys by comparison.

She knew that without a doubt then.

None of them had ever made her want like this, so much she could barely stop the noises tearing from her throat.

"Mmmm," Silas purred, dropping his head down the line of her body. "Fuck me, keep moaning, baby."

She didn't have the words to tell him she couldn't stop, even if she'd tried. The pleasure inside her was too much. She had to let it out, allow it to course through her and then out into the universe somehow. When he reached her hips, he shoved her legs open, gripping both her ass cheeks in his hands and spreading her like he was hungry and she was his Christmas feast.

A present only he got to unwrap.

His eyes raked over her, golden wolf irises glowing in the darkness as he took in every inch of her folds. "So pretty. So sweet. Like candy made for me." He ran a finger down the seam of her slit and she shivered. The way he whispered it, he sounded almost...reverent with appreciation over her, before a twisted smirk pulled at his lips. "Which part of you should I tongue fuck first?" he growled.

Cheyenne let out a harsh hiss at the sudden change. The surprise twist.

His words and that grin were all filth, but she was here for it. It filled her with need.

She couldn't bring herself to answer. Instead, she whimpered a little, sounding like a way sexier version of herself than she'd ever known as she scooted down the bed closer toward him. She watched him lick his lips, like he couldn't wait to get his mouth on her. She knew the feeling, wanted to tell him she felt the same, but she was beyond words at this point.

"I could start with your clit. That'd really make you scream." He dipped his head, flicking his tongue over the sweet bead there. Cheyenne felt herself nearly come up off the bed, as her back arched into him. How could her body even *feel* like that?

No one had ever put their mouth on her there before.

She'd been too nervous to let them, but with Silas she was anything but nervous.

She was alive, wild.

"Or maybe the tight little bud of your ass," he crooned. "I bet you've never let anyone fuck you there. It'd be just for me." He lifted her then, circling his tongue over her back entrance until her legs started to shake. Cheyenne gasped, sputtered. Who even *did* that? Was that *allowed*? Her eyes flew wide open.

He was right. No one had ever touched her there either. She didn't know how to tell him that, or that she didn't even know doing *that*, kissing *there* was even a thing. It wasn't like she'd ever watched human porn or anything. But now that he was doing it, she wanted every part of it. Of him.

She wanted him *everywhere*.

As if he knew it, Silas growled his approval. "Or I could go straight where I want to be and lick your pussy until you're dripping." His nose nudged against her entrance, like he was breathing her scent in. The whiskers on his cheeks brushed against her sensitive skin of her thighs and the contrast surprised her, caught her off guard, but then his tongue plunged into her, full and distracting, stealing all sense from her head before he pulled back. "Fuck, your taste was made for me." A dark fire burned in his eyes from where he smirked at her. "You're mine the rest of the night."

Mine. The possession in that word vibrated through her.

She wanted it, craved it, and yet . . .

"Tonight only," she breathed. The words were out before she could will them back.

Silas froze. Staring up at her like he wasn't exactly pleased about that. "Don't fuck with me like that," he snarled, lip curling.

"I'm not-I'm not fucking with you," she said, trying to understand his meaning. "It's true. I'm leaving," she blurted out. Her admission smashed the tension between them like a sledgehammer, destroying everything. She didn't know why she felt the need to tell him that then, now, but her brain was reeling, telling her she needed to make this more . . . more . . . normal somehow.

More routine.

Every relationship she'd ever had ended shortly after sex. She always figured that she must not have been very good at it, or that her reactions to things, her autism, a part of her she couldn't separate from herself, made her undesirable somehow. Normally, she could hide it away, mask her more neurodiverse behaviors, but she couldn't hide the longer a relationship went on, especially while being intimate. With all the sounds, feelings, sensations. It left her with no place to go. And keeping a relationship to one night only was what people said when they didn't want sex to mean anything, right?

She didn't *want* sex with Silas not to mean anything, but she had to say it before *he* did, because, of course he'd say it. Every one of her other partners did. And it was true. She *was* leaving. That was her plan, which meant she had to stick to it.

"I'm leaving for MAC-V-Alpha just after Christmas," she said.

The phrase settled in the ether between them.

"The military?" Silas brow crinkled as he pulled away from her thighs.

"Yes," she nodded. "A shifters-only unit."

Silas scowled.

She didn't think she'd ever seen him look as grumpy as he did then. Which meant she needed to fix this. Smooth things over.

She scrambled to explain. "I'll be able to use my mechanical skills. All day long. That's why I didn't want to miss the shift-and-run tomorrow. This Christmas is my last one at Wolf Pack Run."

Silas was on his feet then, pacing the room. Every muscle in his corded form seemed to ripple, writhe. "Why are you telling me this? Why now?"

"Because ... I ... " Cheyenne sat up on the bed, clutching the sheet to her chest. "I guess I wanted to be honest. Up front."

Silas stood there for a moment, hands on the narrowed triangle of his hips. Hips that led down to an impressive length. Even partly flaccid as he was now, he was still a sight to behold. He watched her through the glow of the moonlight. "You don't belong in the military."

She didn't know why, but the words stung. "Well, I'm going to belong there. I love working on things."

"And the violence? The fighting?" he nearly snarled. Gold eyes flashed.

Cheyenne's thoughts quickened as she struggled to explain. To be honest, she hadn't really thought about those parts of it until now, but she supposed she could handle it. She'd mostly be working on their machinery anyway. Back at the base. Burying herself in the thing that she loved. Maybe then, if she was a part of a team, had a place, a purpose, she wouldn't feel so separate from everyone else.

So alone.

She shrugged. "Whatever it is, I'll handle it."

"You'll handle it?" he asked. "Christ, Cheyenne. Like you handled tonight?"

"That's not fair." Cheyenne recoiled. "Don't be cruel."

"I'm not trying to be, Cheyenne." He shook his head. "I'm being honest. You don't belong in the military."

"Then where do I belong, Silas?" She glared at him. "You tell me."

~

You belong with me.

Those are the words he wanted to say, but he was too much of chicken shit to say it. Too new at this. Too afraid that if he put it out there in the open between them, she'd say something else that changed everything. This was all moving so fast. Faster than he'd ever anticipated, and already she'd turned him inside out, made him want things he didn't even know he'd needed until now. *What's one more thing?* something inside him asked.

But hard as he tried, he couldn't bring himself to voice it.

Not now that he knew she was leaving.

Not now that he knew like everything else in his life, she was going to break his heart.

He couldn't let her. Not here. Not in this place. Not this close to Christmas.

He already loathed this time of year for good reason. If she broke his heart now, this time he wasn't certain he'd survive it.

"You're right," he said. "Your choices are none of my business."

She nodded, agreeing with him, before she moved to settle in beneath the covers again, like they were finished. Far from it.

He wasn't through with her yet.

"But that doesn't mean you can't still be mine for tonight."

He gripped her by both ankles and pulled, yanking her to the end of the bed in one rough tug. Cheyenne let out a startled squeak. High-pitched and adorable. But she wouldn't sound cute by the time he was done with her. He'd fuck that sunshine right out of her until nothing but pure sex was left, everything she was trying to hide by pushing him away.

The irony that he'd done the same when she'd kissed him didn't escape him.

Positioning her ass near the end of the bed, he dropped to his knees, burying his face there. This wasn't about him. This is about her. Letting her know what she'd been missing. What she'd still miss if she left. Not that he wasn't getting his own twisted joy out of this.

The taste of her pussy on his tongue was fucking exquisite. Better than any sugary treat he'd ever known. Gingerbread. Candy canes. Name it and she tasted better. Like every sweet he'd ever seen as a child sitting in a frosted bakery window.

Sumptuous. Mouthwatering. Unreachable.

He tongued her sweet folds, his cock throbbing with need again as she started to rock against him, finding a rhythm all her own. "That's it, baby. Take what you need."

She was getting wetter by the minute. He felt her pussy pulse as she drew near.

"Silas," she breathed, gasping.

"Yeah, sweetheart?" he purred against her.

"I-I've never came in front of someone before."

Silas froze, paused where he sucked her clit momentarily as he gazed up at her. He wanted to take every asshole she'd been with before and bury them six feet under beneath the snow. He growled. "It's okay, baby. I've got you," he whispered against her. "We don't finish until you're satisfied." He drew her back into his mouth then, the absence having given her just long enough to recover as he ramped the pressure up.

Cheyenne writhed beneath him, fisting the sheets until she was on the verge of ecstasy. But she needed something more to tip her over the edge. Get her out of her own head. He could feel it. He positioned two fingers outside her entrance, prepared to push up, before he nudged his pinky near her back entrance. "This okay?" he asked.

Cheyenne nodded, panting with need.

He entered her all at once, taking her until she bucked against him. She moaned, coming apart on a loud mewl of pleasure. He was lapping her up, reveling in the scent, the smell, the taste of her. Until he was slowly guiding her back down again, bringing her back to earth. He pulled her into his arms, into his lap where he sat on the floor. She belonged there, whether she liked that damn chair of hers or not. He claimed her lips then, kissing her deep as she sunk against him, all loose limbs and shuddered aftershocks.

"That was . . ." She whispered against him, trying to catch her breath. "Best sex of my life," she admitted.

Silas chuckled, appreciating the raw honesty. He gifted her a slow, easy grin. "Baby, I'm not nearly through with you yet." He stood then, lifting her up and into his arms before they both fell onto the bed. "I promise to get you home by morning," he whispered into the crook of her neck and she relaxed against him. "But I can't promise we'll get much sleep."

8

They'd forgotten her.

Cheyenne glanced around the mostly empty cabins of Wolf Pack Run, trying desperately to understand. They always left at the same time. Seven in the morning sharp the day before Christmas Eve. Yet, where there should have been life, cheer, movement, the sounds and laughter of the pack preparing for the holiday, the whole of Wolf Pack Run sat nearly empty. The cabins and halls of the main compound were decorated for Christmas, festive, like they were supposed to be, but there were few left to enjoy them. Only a handful of the children, too young to participate, and the elders responsible for their care. No members of the pack her age.

No one but her anyway.

That morning, when she'd woken, alone in the cabin with Silas, she hadn't been worried, or nervous about making it back. He'd promised her he would get her there in time, despite all odds. She trusted him. Believed. Instead of worrying, she'd stretched out her spent muscles like a cat, long and languid and satisfied. She hadn't fallen asleep until the early hours not long before sunrise, having stayed awake for the best of reasons long into the night, but the sleep she *had* gotten had been some of the best in her life.

There was no weighted blanket that could ever compare to the feeling of Silas' arms around her, the pressure of his broad shoulders, the warmth of his skin. He'd made certain to wake her not long after the sun came up fully. Had even volunteered to stay awake and watch the sunrise to be certain they knew when it was time to go.

He'd woken her softly, gently, far more gentle than he gave himself credit for, stroking his fingers through her hair and watching the way the red strands caught like fire in the morning light. Lying there in his arms, she'd felt happy, sated, content.

More whole than she had in a long time.

But that had all ended the moment they'd stepped out into the cold. The ride back to Wolf Pack Run had been a long one, filled with a heavy silence that seemed to stretch as far as the endless Montana sky. Normally, she would have enjoyed the quiet, but as soon as the truck's engine rumbled to life the silence that'd descended as soon as they'd left the cabin felt... heavy, cold. Final, even. Like whatever waited for them back at Wolf Pack Run neither of them really wanted it. But she'd craved her routine, and he'd promised to have her home on time.

And he did.

It'd taken some time for them to dig their way out of the cabin of course—Silas had needed to pry open a frozen window and shift into his wolf form to dig away the snow that barred the door with his paws. But they'd made it back to Wolf Pack Run with only minutes to spare. Yet still, they'd forgotten her. Left early without her.

Cheyenne stood alone in the empty stillness of her cabin, staring at the cold fire grate for a long time, uncertain what to do with herself. She played over the events of the last twenty-four hours in her head, over and over again, trying to figure out why the pack hadn't left on time, why she'd felt so gutted before they'd even arrived, but she couldn't understand. She was fine. Really. It was okay. If this was her last Christmas at Wolf Pack Run, so be it.

She didn't mind. Being alone with the elders and children was what she was used to. She didn't even mind the change of plans, the disruption in routine. Not this time. Because, if she was honest with herself, she'd expected it. She'd known from the moment they'd been snowed in.

Because to her disappointment...

It wasn't even the first time they'd left her.

∼

WHAT THE *FUCK* had Maverick been thinking?

Silas prowled around the empty compound, speculating what had been going through the packmaster's mind, but he couldn't begin to understand it. Not without thoroughly wanting to tear the Grey Wolf leader in two anyway. Not only had the pack not left on time—goddamn early even—not bothering to question why he or Cheyenne hadn't arrived back yet, but the wolves they *had* left were only a handful of the pack's newest warriors, young alpha males practically still in training. Only a handful of them, to protect *all* of the compound *and* all of the elder wolves and children of the pack, those too ancient, too young, or no longer able bodied to complete the run, along with a few past retired warriors who were physically disabled and handful of others who didn't want to participate.

What in the flying fuck?

Silas snarled, his anger warring inside him as he tore into the main hall, trying to parse out his next move. At least they'd had the damn decency to keep the security room locked, like that did a whole lot of fucking good when the whole of the ranch was vulnerable. He was by far the most skilled warrior here, the fiercest and most trained, so the moment he'd assessed the situation, Grey Wolf or not, he'd immediately taken charge. No one had even questioned it.

When he hadn't been able to open the security room door immediately with an old kitchen knife, he'd quickly destroyed the handle with the blunt end of a horse shoe. None of the young warriors or others left behind had seemed to know where to locate the key or even a hammer or something to take the door off its hinges and Cheyenne and her tools seemed to have disappeared into the ranch's ether shortly after they'd arrived.

Silas froze where he stood in the security office, pouring over the pack's monitor screens. There was nothing important of note there...yet. But...

Fucking hell.

Cheyenne.

His mind raced. She'd be alone. Devastated at being left behind. Maybe even having another anxiety attack or... whatever that was yesterday. He wanted to go to her, hold her again. She'd told him one night only. Made where they stood abundantly clear.

He had to respect that, listen, didn't he? Even though leaving everything they'd shared behind in his family's old cabin this morning had nearly done him in.

Goddamnit. *His family.* Silas' hands clenched into fists.

If losing Cheyenne so soon after he'd found her hadn't thoroughly destroyed him, being in that cabin again would have. She'd been the perfect distraction, something he could focus on, and yet... She was so much more than that.

Fuck, he loved her, didn't it? He didn't even know when or where it started, it'd happened so fast, but he did. She'd just suddenly become a part of him. Like his wolf or a limb or piece of him he hadn't known he'd been missing. He couldn't separate it out from the rest of himself. She lit him up like the morning sunrise, filling in all the cracks and darkness.

Damn it, he couldn't let her go.

She didn't belong in MAC-V-Alpha or the military or whatever the hell she thought she was running off to like that would solve all her troubles. She belonged with him. He just had to make her see it. At least tell her he loved her before he let her say goodbye.

And fuck. Tomorrow would be Christmas. The fifteen-year anniversary of when those bloodsuckers had stolen everything from him, and Maverick had left him this, this place, abandoned.

As open and unprotected as he and his family had been fifteen years earlier.

His sisters and brothers. His father. His mother.

All gone, and yet, the holiday security plans weren't any better after fifteen fucking years. In the subpacks *or* here. Silas roared his rage into the silence.

Didn't anyone have any sense around here?

By the time his frustration finished ravaging through him and the office, his hands were planted firmly on the security desk. He leaned onto its surface as he used his biceps to support his weight. He was panting, nearly feral with rage.

But needed to calm himself. Handle this. Fix this. Make it right.

He could do that, couldn't he?

"Damn, I thought only the cougar pride could roar like that, but you Wild Eight were always pussies too, I guess." The grating voice and amused snicker that came from behind him caused him to stiffen.

Slowly, Silas turned his head toward the wolf who'd spoken only to find the Asshole whose nose he'd broken staring back at him. Just great.

"You," he grumbled.

"Yeah, me." Asshole shrugged, where he leaned against the doorway.

What had Cheyenne said his name was again? Cayden?

No wonder he was a douchebag. God, what an obnoxious name.

Silas snarled, not bothering to move. "Unless you'd like your nose broken again, or worse," his lip curled, "I suggest you get the fuck out."

He shouldn't have been surprised. Of course, this asshole would have been some untrained little-alpha wolf shit, a newbie barely past his den days. He should've recognized that from the start. No fully fledged Grey Wolf warrior in their right mind would bother Cheyenne. Challenge him. The whole of the pack loved her. Almost as much as they feared him.

Silas turned back toward the security screens, tracking each monitor with careful precision. The pack's security specialist, Blaze, had the ranch perimeter well covered, but with this few warriors to man the posts, they'd be vulnerable for the next several days.

And his and Cheyenne's near-run in with the vamps in Missoula still didn't sit right.

"Unfortunately, you're stuck with me," Cayden said from the doorway.

Silas snarled. "The fuck I am."

"He could feel the other wolf hesitate. Sense him there. "Maverick got word of what I said about Cheyenne."

Silas looked toward the other wolf again.

"A broken nose doesn't go unnoticed around here for long." Cayden frowned.

"And what did your packmaster say to you?" Silas asked through gritted teeth.

He wasn't sure he wanted to know the answer based on the

mess of the pack's current security plans, but something compelled him to ask anyway.

Hope, he quickly realized. Identifying the emotion. Cheyenne had filled him with it.

It'd been the first time he'd felt it in a long, long time.

"Maverick said you were right. Laid into me. Gave me a thorough talking to," Cayden answered. "Tasked me with going out and looking for you after the storm cleared, but I did you a solid, man, and told him him you were holed up with Cheyenne." Cayden winked. "Guess I was right."

Silas snarled. So that was why no one had came looking for them. Why no one had picked up their phones this morning, because this asshole had lied and said they were fine when he hadn't even bothered to search or confirm.

They could have still been stuck in that cabin. Or worse...

"Don't you dare speak her name again," Silas advanced on him, teeth bare. "You're not worthy of it." Of her. This little shit never would be.

Cayden threw up his hands in surrender. "Look, I was drunk before, being a douche, but I didn't realize she was autistic, okay? There's a lot of members of this pack, man. It's a lot to keep track of and—"

Silas didn't hear the rest of what the coward was saying because his mind was too busy reeling again. Suddenly, it all made sense. Cheyenne's tender-hearted trust in him. Her willingness to take him at his word, believe. Her love of fairness, equity, her routines. The way she talked about textures and sensations like they were different from her, sometimes too much. Even the way she treated her tools. The way she laughed when she was nervous. Hell, even her blunt claim on the chair.

For a brief moment, Silas couldn't breathe.

And he'd fucked her six ways till Sunday, taken her in ways she'd flat out told him no one had touched her before. His heart reeled. Did that mean he'd taken advantage of her? Her innocence? Her naivety? She couldn't read other people's emotions as well as he could.

But he hadn't known...

No.

No, he quickly decided.

Just because she was a woman with autism didn't mean she wasn't her own person, an adult allowed to make her choices. She'd been just as into everything they'd done as he had been. But he could have been more gentle with her—emotionally. Physically.

Fuck, he was an ass.

Cayden was still talking, rambling now even. "But Maverick left me here as punishment, told me to make amends."

"What did you say?"

"I said Maverick left me here as punishment and—"

"No. No before that." It still hadn't sunk in. He needed to hear it again. Confirmation he'd heard correctly.

Cayden paused, watching the realization dawn on Silas' face. "You didn't know?"

Silas didn't answer. Just shook his head.

"I can smell her on you." Cayden wrinkled his nose pointedly like he could tell everything that had happened between them. Likely could. Silas hadn't showered since. "You disappointed?"

"No." Silas shook his head again. "Never."

It didn't change anything. Not the way he felt about her. None of it.

Sure, it definitely explained some things. But it didn't change a goddamn thing about how he felt.

"Good, because that wouldn't be cool, man."

Silas shot the other wolf a glare. He was good and tired of this annoying motherfucker.

Cayden threw up his hands like he realized what Silas was thinking. "Look I know I was a jerk before, but I'm going to apologize, okay? I never would have said that if I'd known."

Silas growled. "Doesn't matter if you knew or not. You were an asshole all the same."

And so was he. In the beginning at least, though she'd quickly worked her way into his heart. Silas' eyes went wide. Is *that* why she wanted to join the military, MAC-V? To belong? Because here on the ranch, she didn't feel understood, seen, and the military was a place that thrived on forced teamwork, routine, where she could do what she loved all day, hyper-focus, and not have to explain? Or had she thought if he'd known she was autistic that maybe he wouldn't want her? That maybe they'd be over? So she'd ended it, ended them, before it even really began?

When she'd told him one night only, it'd sounded like she was repeating a phrase she'd no doubt heard before. One that'd been used to hurt her. Even as she'd said it, it hadn't sounded like her. Didn't have her same positivity. That shimmer and shine he'd come to associate with her. The phrase had seemed ... foreign on her lips. Like she'd panicked and didn't know what to do with it.

Shit.

"Maverick also said that when you got back you were in charge. Said you'd know what to do," Cayden shrugged, drawing his attention again. "Guess he doesn't care you used to be Wild Eight. Just like Wes."

Silas shook his head, barely registering that he was answering. "No. No, it's not the same."

This. This was the trust test.

Not just protecting Cheyenne. But protecting the ranch, getting her to stay. The pack would never want her to leave. All of it. The tasks were one and the same.

Take care of her, he could hear the packmaster saying it clearly in his mind's eye now.

Though admittedly, Silas had failed the first part. Hadn't left her untouched. But he and the packmaster were going to have a little discussion about that, about female packmembers making their own choices, especially marginalized ones, *and* about the holes in the holiday security, whenever the pack returned. But until then...

"I have to make this right."

9

It was well past dark by the time anyone came looking for her. A knock rapped at her cabin door, sharp and quick. Cheyenne laid on her bed, beneath one of her weighted blankets, staring up at the ceiling. Whoever it was, she didn't want to answer. She didn't have to, did she?

No one could *make* her come out.

She debated for several moments until finally social obligation won. Her mother would have told her to answer it. That was the polite, *acceptable* thing to do. The *normal* thing. Wiggling from beneath her blanket, she padded across the cold hard wood floors, thankful for the seamless red and green Christmas socks she'd put on. They made it feel like her feet were snuggled into a warm, tight cocoon, but still kept her toes free.

She made her way to the door.

When she opened it, Silas stood on the other side, waiting for her. Standing there in the moonlight, his Stetson tipped low over his face and a fitted leather jacket covering his arms, she could hardly believe he'd wanted her enough the night before to do the things they had. She blushed slightly.

She was still a bit sore today, a steady, welcome kind of ache.

One that reminded her every time she moved of all the ways he stole her breath away.

He flashed her devious grin.

She blinked at him, uncertain what to do—he'd never come to her cabin *before*. Once they'd parted ways this morning, she hadn't expected him to ever look at her with more than a passing glance. That's what any other cowboy wolf on this ranch would do. Brag about the fact they'd slept with her, because she was objectively good looking. A bombshell. Whatever *that* meant. Her last partner had said so anyway. Maybe they'd even felt proud of themselves for being progressive, like sleeping with the autistic girl was some fun novelty, before they promptly forgot about her.

But Silas hadn't forgotten her. Not today.

He leaned one large arm over the entryway, his biceps straining against his leather in a way that drew far too much of her attention as he watched her. An appreciative rumble sounded low in his throat as his gaze raked over her, before settling on where her bare toes peeped out from her seamless socks. He bit his lower lip for a moment, before he visibly swallowed, but she wasn't certain whether he was trying not to growl in appreciation or laugh at her outrageous socks. Finally, he cleared his throat. "I came to save Christmas."

Cheyenne stared up at him, blinking. He was so tall he'd have to duck to come through the doorway, but while she appreciated his directness, she still didn't know what he meant. "Does Christmas *need* saving?" She lifted a brow.

Silas smirked a little at that, amused. "What I mean is that I know you're disappointed the pack left you behind and I want to make you feel better," he explained. "By doing . . . " He cringed a little like something he was about to say pained him. "Christmas things with you."

On his tongue, the word Christmas sounded like a curse word.

Cheyenne wasn't certain what to make of that.

She stepped to the side, letting him come through the door as she retreated into the warmth of her cabin. She heard the door close behind him, but she was too busy shaking her head, not looking at him. She didn't think she had it in her to try and maintain eye contact right now. She was struggling today. Unable to mask in her usual way.

"You don't have to do that, Silas. I—" Her voice trailed off as she tried to explain. "Sometimes . . . Sometimes Christmas is overwhelming for me anyways. The lights. The music. It's all a bit much. Unless I brace myself for it." All true, but she also loved Christmas when it didn't overwhelm her. But that part she failed to say.

"I know," he said. "I know, Cheyenne."

She turned to look at him then. Watched his face for a beat. As long as she could without feeling uncomfortable. It felt like there was something *more* to his words, if she was reading him correctly, which she probably wasn't. "What do you mean?"

Silas pawed at the back of his neck, glanced down briefly. "I know that you're . . ." His voice trailed off.

The words her brain supplied to finish that sentence weren't entirely kind. All things that'd been said to her over the years. Things her brain had put on repeat. An endless loop of people who'd hurt her, treated her as less than.

"Do you prefer autistic or a person with autism?" Silas asked, abruptly.

Cheyenne blinked, stunned a bit. No one had ever cared to ask her before. She paused long enough to consider. "Autistic please," she whispered. "My autism isn't separate from the rest of me."

This meant he wouldn't want her anymore, didn't it? Now that he knew. If he hadn't decided that already.

She turned away from him. "How did you know?" she asked, making her way to her kitchen. She reached into her cabinet, grabbing a mug shaped like a chubby little penguin wearing a Christmas scarf from the cabinet and holding it up to offer him coffee or tea. That's what she was supposed to do when people came over.

Offer them a hot beverage. Or food.

Silas shook his head, frowning at the mug slightly. "Cayden told me." He grimaced a little as he said the other wolf's name. "But I had my suspicions before that."

She set the penguin mug on the empty countertop. "I guess I'm not very good at masking."

"Why should you be?" Silas sounded like he was . . . maybe offended? On her behalf. "There's nothing wrong with you, Cheyenne." He paused, the muscles in his throat moving. "You're perfect."

Cheyenne suddenly couldn't breathe again. When she recovered, she breathed out a long sigh before she busied herself by reaching into the cabinet for a packet of hot cocoa mix. She hated the bitterness of coffee and tea was like drinking dirty leaf water. "That's a kind thing to say, but you don't have to do that."

"Do what?"

"Pretend like it doesn't bother you." She shrugged. "Like it doesn't change how you feel about me."

"It doesn't." Silas didn't hesitate. "That's what I came to show you."

Cheyenne clutched hold of the penguin mug, anchoring herself. "Please don't lie to me. I . . . as you already said, I'm too trusting."

"I'm not lying, Cheyenne. Promise." He removed his Stetson

from his head, glancing at her earnestly. "Please believe me. You did before."

She turned on the burner, watching it so she could catch the water before it let out that awful screech. Her distorted reflection stared back at her from its chrome surface. "Even if that's the case, I'm still leaving. For MAC-V-Alpha."

"I'm hoping I can change your mind about that, and even if I can't, we can make it work." Silas' hand touched her side now, making her jump slightly. He mumbled a gruff apology as he turned her and pulled her against him, nestling her against his hips, as he pressed her to him. He was solid there, on his stomach, his chest. All over. Hard and sturdy. And as he dropped his head down into her hair to bury his face in it, she felt the hardened length beneath the fly of his jeans press against her belly.

He wasn't lying. He still wanted her.

"You mean ... ?" Cheyenne couldn't stop the hope that snuck into her voice.

"I don't want to push you into anything you're not ready for, but ... " He lifted her chin, tilting her head up toward him. "Can you just put on your coat and come with me? Please. I'll get on my knees and beg if I have to, sweetheart."

Cheyenne giggled. There was something extremely funny to her about the idea of seeing this enormous cowboy, her pack's former enemy, get on his knees for anyone. Though she supposed he'd already done that for her the night before. Heat filled her cheeks again. "I don't feel like horseback riding right now." She'd seen his horse, reins tied up on her fence post, outside when he'd arrived. She loved horses, animals, but it also reminded her of therapy.

"Could you please make this easy on me?" He chuckled. "I'm begging you, Chey. Just get on the damn horse, woman." He grumbled against her hair.

The kettle screeched. She jumped, started to cover her ears, but he snatched it off the stove so quickly, the sound disappeared in seconds. He switched the burner off.

She smiled up at him. He really was trying. "Okay." She nodded. "Okay."

He took her hand in his then, making her forget all about the cocoa as he led her toward the door. "You've trusted me from the start. All I'm asking you to do is keep trusting me."

∼

THEY RODE out together in the snow, Cheyenne nestled in front of him in the saddle seat. It was coming down softly now. Slow and easy. The chill of the night created fully formed crystals that got caught in her hair. She looked like a glittering vision in the moonlight, some kind of adorable little Christmas faerie. Lord knew she had the effortlessly cute features for it.

Silas wrapped an arm around her, pulling closer where she was settled against him. Having the curved peach of her ass right up on him for the better part of an hour wasn't doing a damn thing for his self-control, and he felt his wolf stir in awareness. But he was trying to be patient. Not push her into anything. He'd wait for her to come to him. Whenever she was ready.

Before they'd left, she'd insisted she could ride her own horse. Oreo was its name apparently. When he'd asked her, "why Oreo?" she'd simply shrugged and said she liked cookies, which didn't surprise him in the least, considering she always smelled like vanilla and sugar. Fitting for a woman so sweet. But he'd insisted they ride together.

He wanted to keep her close, warm, happy.

Whatever she needed him to be.

"This isn't the first time they've left me," she said suddenly, her breath swirling around him into the ether. The forest was dark, still, filled with the kind of quiet only created by the falling snow. They were nearly three-quarters of the way to their destination, and they'd spent most of the ride in companionable silence. A different kind from how the truck ride been this morning. More comfortable. There weren't any secrets between them any longer.

Nothing to hide.

He liked that.

"The first time?" he mumbled, careful to keep his voice low since he was speaking directly into her ear. "Was it intentional?" He didn't know what he might do to her packmates if it was, but he couldn't consider that at the moment.

All he could consider was letting her talk, heal.

Cheyenne shook her head. "I don't know. Intention is hard for me to understand."

"Why don't you explain it to me?" he whispered, urging her on.

Maybe talking to him would help her make sense of it. From the way the words had fallen out of her, so fast and abruptly, like they couldn't wait to escape a moment longer, he got the impression this was something she needed to get off her chest.

"There's not much to tell. I was a teenager. Maybe fourteen. It was supposed to be the first year I went on the shift-and-run. But I didn't mature, emotionally I mean, as fast as other girls. I was angry at my mother for something. I can't even remember what. But I was having a bit of a meltdown. Probably over something she thought was silly, but it wasn't to me. It was Christmas. I was overwhelmed, overstimulated, but she told me if I couldn't," she made air quotes with her hands, "'cut my attitude' to go sulk in my room the whole time."

"And?"

"And I did. I didn't know what cutting attitude meant or how to stop being me, so when I didn't show up for the shift-and-run on time, everyone thought just I didn't want to participate that year. Back then I tended to have more meltdowns around the holidays anyway, so I guess they just sort of figured I would take care of myself? Since I was a teen after all..." She shrugged as if it wasn't a big thing, a huge ask of an autistic fourteen-year-old. "I sat alone in my room for two days waiting for them to come back. To come and get me. Like my mother told me to do."

"Jesus," Silas swore.

"I take things pretty literally. Even more then than now. I've gotten better at hiding it, I guess." She sighed. "I was diagnosed shortly after that. The pack doctors weren't really sure what to do with me. It's not like autism is that common among our kind."

"More common than you'd think."

She glanced over her shoulder to look at him, silently asking.

"My younger brother," he clarified with a shrug of his own. "But it was a long time ago and he was a kid at the time, so I-I didn't recognize it with you at first."

"Gender is a diagnosis barrier," she said, like she was reading the line aloud from a textbook. "People expect autism to occur more in boys than girls. We get diagnosed less."

"I'm sorry that happened to you," he whispered. "That the pack didn't recognize it sooner, I mean."

"Maverick became packmaster not long after that. He made things better. Made certain there were accommodations for me. Support. I'd been trying to work myself up to going with them after that. No longer staying behind with the children. I'd told Maverick I thought I could finally handle it this year." She hesitated. "Except that they forgot me again. They probably thought I'd changed my mind and didn't want to go."

"I'm sure there's a reason," Silas muttered. "More than that." Other than Cayden, though he wasn't about to explain that at present. And if there *wasn't* a good reason he and his new packmaster were going to have a problem. A big one. One that could only be solved with his canine teeth sinking into the other wolf.

A beat of silence passed between them.

"Where are we headed?" Cheyenne asked, finally.

The gentle sway of his horse beneath them was calm, steady. There was no hurry. They had all night and already they were almost there.

"You'll see."

A way ahead, a clearing in the trees parted to reveal one of the Grey Wolves' guest halls, a massive several story mansion of a cabin buried in the woods, used to house other shifter clans, a whole pack, when they came to stay for Seven Range Pact business. Several lights glowed inside, where a few members of the pack were still awake. He'd relocated them there as soon as possible, once he'd made certain it was secure, safe.

"Why are we here?" Cheyenne asked.

"I'll explain once we're inside." When his horse finally moseyed to a halt, he dismounted, lifting Cheyenne down from the horse and passing the reins off to one of the young alpha wolves he'd designated to play stable hand while they were out there.

Silently, he took Cheyenne's hand and led her inside. He hadn't known whether it was better to warn her or surprise her for this, but he thought maybe he'd chosen right from the sparkle in her wide eyes. A sharp intake of breath came from her lips.

The inside of the cabin had been decorated to the nines. Every elegant Christmas decoration he'd been able to haul out from the pack's storage. He'd spent the whole of the day doing it, enlisting the help of her few remaining packmates, until the cabin practically glittered inside. He'd taken care to keep the lights dim, cozy. Enough to impress, but not enough that it would overwhelm her, overstimulate, he hoped.

Silas grumbled, uncertain what to say now that he had her there by his side. "I figured if you couldn't stick to your old routines, we'd make new ones. New memories. Ones you could do any time you wanted. With or without your packmates." He gave a rough clear of his throat, willing the words out. "I want you to stay, Cheyenne," he admitted. "I don't want you to go off to MAC-V-Alpha or the military or wherever. I know you haven't signed your papers yet, and I want you here. With me." He swore under his breath. "Fuck, I don't think I've ever wanted anything more."

Cheyenne stepped further into the room, staring up at the towering pine he and several of the Grey Wolf warriors had chopped down for the tree. It'd been a total bitch to get through the door, but somehow they'd managed. Several storage containers filled with decorations sat off to the side, waiting to be used in the morning.

For a moment, he stood watching Cheyenne slowly place her hand on one of the pine branches, tentatively feeling the nettles. "I don't know what to say," she breathed. She looked him straight in the eye then. "You did all this for me?"

He nodded. "For you, and some others." He pawed a hand over the hair on his face. It was getting a bit long. He needed a damn shave. "Being here, centralized in one place makes security easier for those of you still here. Those bloodsuckers are less likely to pick your packmates off like flies if we're all together like this. I tried to keep that in mind."

She was still watching him, not glancing away now. A subtle sheen shimmered in her eyes. "I don't understand half of what you just said, but I don't care." She ran toward him then, launched herself into his arms, wrapping her arms around his neck and kissing his face.

He chuckled. "I'll try to keep the idioms to a minimum." Lifting her by her delicious bottom, he scooped her into his arms, settling her legs around his waist, before he carried her up the stairs to where the bedrooms waited.

Once they'd reached the door to her room, he kissed her, slow and deep, a long mingling of tongues until all he could taste was her. God, she tasted sweet. Like every dessert he'd ever wanted but had denied himself out of concern, principle. When they finally pulled back, her lips were swollen, her nose pink and flushed from where every part of them that'd been cold had grown warm.

"Get some sleep," he muttered, setting her on her feet and stepping back. He nodded to the bedroom at their right, one he'd been certain to fill with several of her weighted blankets he'd snuck out of the pack's clean laundry room. "We've got a full schedule in the morning. There's a note on your beside with everything we're doing. I know it's not a part of your usual Christmas routine, but I'd hoped if I told you what was going to happen beforehand, that'd help you prepare for it." He glanced at his feet. "I'm sorry it's not what you'd planned for."

"No. No, don't apologize." Cheyenne smiled at him. That bright sunshiny grin beamed brighter than any Christmas lights he'd ever seen. "It's perfect. Thank you."

Silas nodded his gratitude. Hesitated, then grumbled a goodnight he didn't want to say, before turning away. He didn't expect her to answer him yet, decide if she'd stay right away. He wouldn't pressure her. He was halfway down the hall before she called after him.

"Silas?"

He turned toward her. Fuck, she was breathtaking. A ray of light in his dark. He didn't know how he'd ever pushed away from her. How he'd ever let her go. No doubt that time would come. She still wasn't for him. Not really. Even though he'd been letting himself pretend.

"Do you . . . ?" Cheyenne wrung her hands together, looking up at him through those long, lush eyelashes, only to blush. The fact that she could after all the things she'd done with him nearly did him in. He wanted to take her right there, in the hall, out in the open. Bend her over the railing for all to see. Claim her as his own.

She's not yours to claim.

He watched her hesitate. "Whatever it is, you can ask me."

"Do you think I could sleep with you?" Cheyenne's blush deepened a little. "In your bed, I mean?"

Silas felt himself shudder with relief. "I was afraid you'd never ask." He swept her into his arms, causing her to let a giggling squeal. Wasting no time, he kicked open her door, whisking her inside. Another night without sleep would leave them both tired, but fuck, he was going to make it worth it.

10

How he was ever going to live without her, Silas didn't know. He sat in the pack's guest hall kitchen, perched at the marble-topped island counter on one of several wooden stools. The apron Cheyenne had tied on him, a red and green gingham patterned atrocity, which apparently belonged to the pack's security specialist, Blaze, read: "On the Naughty List. I regret nothing." He glanced down at the lettering again, frowning at the sight. He was covered in flour by now, patches of it coating him from nearly head to toe. There was even a bit in his hair, his beard, not to mention the mess of sticky icing on his hands.

The warm scent of cinnamon, clove, and ginger mixed with peppermint buttercream filled the air, permeating the room. They were alone now and had been for hours, leaving an unwelcome, quiet tension between them. The gingerbread panels which they'd been working on for the better part of the afternoon had finally cooled, and now, much to his chagrin, she expected him to assemble it and *decorate* for fuck's sake.

Silas stared down at the crumbling mess that was supposed to be his gingerbread house, feeling it collapse further beneath his rough hands. It kept crumbling beneath his fingertips, which he only now realized were rather large, blunt. Overtly masculine. Like they belonged to the cowboy he'd become.

Why the fuck did people enjoy doing this?

He grimaced. "I don't think I'm doing it right."

Cheyenne didn't bother to look toward him. "It's easy. Just follow the directions." She waved a dismissive hand.

He *had*. Or tried to, at least, and look where the hell that'd gotten him.

Silas glanced down at the monstrosity he'd created again. His gingerbread house looked more like gingerbread rubble. Or maybe some poor half-hearted attempt at an igloo, if he squinted hard enough. He grunted his displeasure. How was he supposed to convince her to stay if he couldn't even build a damn gingerbread house for her?

He glanced over to Cheyenne's station, where she was still working, entranced in the minutiae and detail of her creation. Whereas his portion of the kitchen island had become chaos shortly after he'd started, bits of icing, flour, candy, and crumbled gingerbread walls scattered all over the place, hers was as neat as a pin. Tidy. Meticulous. Perfect.

He frowned.

She was so good at all this, being a part of a family, a pack, creating new traditions with him that it made his chest ache. How could she not see it?

Just this morning when she'd gathered the elders and children together after breakfast to help her decorate the tree, he'd stood in the shadows by the fireside, watching her. The ease with which the pups and the elders adored her was one he wished she could witness like he did, from the outside looking in. She may have been different from them, but her packmates loved her for it, for her tenderness, her loving heart, the warmth she brought into every shadow near her presence, and while they may not have always been perfect allies, they clearly adored her, accepted her, autism and all. Hell, they gravitated toward the light she provided. Just like he did.

He watched as she squeezed a small dollop of peppermint buttercream from a piping bag onto the roof of her gingerbread house, taking incredible care not to collapse the roof in.

No, gingerbread house wasn't correct. More like gingerbread mansion.

She'd built a veritable castle made of warm, spicy cookie which smelled nearly as delicious and delectable as she did.

Gently, she set down the piping bag and picked up a purple gumdrop only to depress it onto the roof with an almost intense level of precision. Silas grunted again, reaching down to adjust himself and grumbling several profanities under his breath. He'd intended to do all this to bring her closer, make it feel as if she wasn't about to drift away from him, though he knew it was inevitable, and his lower half had gotten the memo. But as he'd watched her that morning, now, he'd never felt further from her than he had then. Never more like an outsider. Someone who didn't deserve her, this place.

Any of it.

There hadn't been cookies and gingerbread houses and tree decorating when he'd been a member of the Wild Eight. Not that he'd wanted there to be. Not like he did now.

"I'm not very good at this," he grumbled again.

"Is there a reason you're being such a Grinch?" She squeezed the piping bag in her hands a little too hard, causing some of the white icing to coat her fingertips.

"A Grinch?"

Cheyenne shrugged. "Yeah, you know, like that human TV Christmas special. The Grinch Who Stole Christmas. He steals Christmas away only to bring it all back and make it better again. I think it was based on a children's book or something."

She tried to wipe at some of the icing on her fingers with her other hand, but it only smeared further. "But even after his heart grows three-sizes larger, I always figured he wouldn't have been very pleased about it."

"I'm not."

But she was right. His heart had grown. She'd made sure of it. She'd worked her way in, filling up parts he hadn't known he needed, longed for, until she'd first kissed him.

"I know." She glanced toward him and made a show of rolling her eyes. "You've made that abundantly clear." She smiled a little.

He glanced around them then, to his crumbling gingerbread mess and the mounds of snow coating the mountainside outside the frosted window. "I hate Christmas," he admitted.

"You hate Christmas?" Cheyenne looked more offended than every time he'd ever swore, before she giggled at him. "That can't be true. You did all this." She waved her piping bag in a circle around them. "Brought us here. What kind of person hates Christmas anyway?"

"One who's never had a family to share it with," he mumbled under his breath, uncertain if she'd heard him. "Not for a long time, that is." He watched as she placed an icing covered finger in her mouth, gently sucking on it. Observing her from a comfortable distance like this had already been getting to him. That cutesy little apron she wore that showed off her curves. The messy bun full of gorgeous red-hair on her head. And now, this...

"Fuck, why do you keep doing that?" He sounded grumpy even to his own ears.

Cheyenne blinked at him innocently. "Doing what?"

Her finger was still poised on her lip, where she was bent over her gingerbread house, flashing a generous amount of cleavage. Like some sexy-as-fuck Christmas pinup.

He tilted his chin toward her. "You know—"

She glanced down at her finger and then her apron, confused. "I *don't* know or I wouldn't have asked you."

He grumbled again. Shit. He was being an ass, thinking she'd automatically realize what he was thinking and now he was going to have to explain it. "That," he nodded to her hand, choosing the least amount of words, the path of least resistant. "You keep licking icing off your finger, and where it gets caught at the sides of your lip."

Cheyenne's hand shot to the side of her perfect, plump mouth. "Do you think I need to be more sanitary?" She looked a bit concerned by that idea, like she'd done something wrong.

"No, it's not that. It's—" Good God, she was making this difficult. He shook his head. No, *he'd* made it difficult by not being clear with her. Direct and forthright like she needed.

She was simply being herself.

He struggled to explain. "After what I said to you last night, I didn't want to push you into anything, force you into any big decisions, but you doing that is making staying away from you . . . difficult." He nearly groaned.

Cheyenne's eyes grew wide. "Oh, you mean in *that* way." A coy smile curled her lips. "I mean, we're alone. That wouldn't be so bad, would it?" She shrugged a little shoulder, batting those wide amber eyes at him.

Silas felt his cock stiffen, and he had to reach down and adjust himself again.

It wouldn't be so bad, except . . .

Except now that he'd seen her with the pack's pups that morning all he could think about, all he'd craved was to fill her up, take her rough and hard, until he spilled his seed into the depths of her womb. Not careful. Not tender like he should be. But a rough, literal claiming. As many times as it took until everyone knew she was his mate. She'd look absolutely scrumptious a few months from now, round and full with his child, something that was wholly theirs, and he wanted that future with her so badly, so keenly, he ached for it.

For future Christmases full of family, one of their creation.

A new life. A better one. Exactly as the packmaster had said. But not with the pack.

With her.

"Cheyenne," he warned, his voice lowering to a gruff rumble. He could see what she was trying to do now and he didn't care for it, or maybe he cared for it *too* much.

His cock ached, balls tightening with need.

"I know what you're thinking," she said, "or at least I think I do, and you don't have to worry." Cheyenne pranced her way around the kitchen island toward him, sauntering with an extra little sway in her hips that made his mouth fucking water. "I already locked the door and hid the key when we came in." She placed a small hand on his chest, and he let out a troubled hiss. That wasn't what he'd been thinking at all. He honestly didn't give a fuck who saw them.

"You naughty, sexy little minx," he purred.

He hauled her up and into his arms, sprawling her out overtop the kitchen island within seconds, careful to stick to his messy side to keep her careful gingerbread creation intact.

She squealed a little, wiggling and playfully swatting at him a bit, as he tore her apron off. Those damn little strings in the back didn't stand a chance against him. Her shirt and pants came next. He bent down, growling against her ear. "You're the only kind of dessert I want to eat." He licked the whorl there. "Now and always."

"What if you did then?"

He pulled back, watched her grin up at him.

"What if you had me exactly how you want me?" She stared up at him with those large doe eyes. "Would that be so bad?"

He groaned. "You're killing me, woman."

"I don't think you mean that literally."

He shook his head, chuckled. "I don't."

"Then what *do* you mean?"

"I mean I want to take you raw, bare, right here against this counter, sweetheart." He drew back, spreading her legs wide. "Fill you up with a different kind of sugar." He dipped a finger into a nearby dollop of icing that'd fallen on the countertop and dangled it over her with that mischievous question in his eyes. A devilish smirk tugged at his lips.

"What if I want the same thing?" She nodded at the icing in his hand, but he knew they were talking about more than that. "What if I said yes?"

"You don't mean that." He shook his head. "Not with me." His eyes flashed to his wolf.

"Don't tell me what I mean, Silas." Her features suddenly hardened, for only a moment, as if she were annoyed by his denial, but the sunshine was back just as quick. "I want you. I want this." She rose up off the table enough to reach down and cup the hard mound straining at the fly of his jeans, where his length threatened to break free. "That's all I want this Christmas," she smiled at him, clearly pleased at her own cleverness at parroting a song. As if he were a gift, a present. But the situation was reversed, couldn't she see?

She was his gift.

Everything he'd ever wanted.

"Please." She bit her lower lip.

And it was about that time Silas lost it.

Fuck, if he'd every really stood a chance of saying no to her in the first place. He growled his pleasure, spreading her further open where she laid on the island counter, naked and bare. He wanted to spoil this woman now and every Christmas for the rest of his goddamn days. Treat her like a queen. Whatever she wanted, needed, he'd give it to her.

Even this.

He was too far gone give to two fucks about the consequences.

Maybe even wanted them, if he was honest with himself.

Crooking his icing covered finger, he made her come closer, painting it over her nipples, the line of her belly. Lower...

"I'm not sure about the texture of that there," she whispered, wiggling a little beneath him. Silas dropped his head, taking one of her ample breasts into his mouth and sucking. Cheyenne gasped, moaned a little. "Never mind," she panted. "I can handle the texture if you keep licking me there."

And he did, over and over until she was moaning, practically keening, both of them wild with need. Pulling back then, he stood over her for a moment, watching as she squirmed in anticipation beneath his gaze. He'd cleared his side of the work station with one shove of his arm across the countertop and he loved the way the mess, the icing and the glistening sheen of where he'd licked it from her left a trail of where he'd been. Not to mention, there was something incredibly sexy about the idea of him taking her, clothes still on, while she was splayed open there.

Slowly, Silas unbuckled his belt, the sound of the leather strap and metal clasp biting through the silence between them. Somewhere off in the distance, on the other side of the cabin, he could hear Christmas music playing, blaring through speakers.

No one would hear them. A good thing considering the noises he knew she would make by the time he was through with her.

Unbuttoning his jeans, he dropped them down to the thick muscles of thighs. Leaving only his dick and a bare bit of ass showing. He took the length of his cock in his hand, working the veined shaft, feeling the girth there, the smooth skin of the head.

"You're certain you want this?"

Every other time he'd taken her, alone in the cabin, and then in her room the night earlier, he'd been certain to wear a condom, or at the very least when they'd been without, he'd pulled out before he'd finished, spending himself on the soft feminine curve of her belly.

This would be different. A raw, wild claiming.

Cheyenne nodded. Bit her lip again. Her folds were glistening, practically dripping for him. "I ache for you there." She snaked a hand down, fingering her own clit.

Silas felt a bead of moisture gather at his tip. "Fuck, baby. I want that too." He gripped her by her hips then, fingers digging into the soft, rounded flesh there as he positioned himself outside her entrance. "I love you," he whispered, daring to say it first as he sheathed himself deep inside her. He may have been clothed, but she'd already laid him bare.

Anyone with eyes could see it.

Cheyenne cried out, surging up against him. He stilled for a moment, letting her adjust to the size of him again, the weight. Reveled in the feel of her fingertips massaging over his scalp, tangling in his hair. "I love you too," she whispered against his cheek. "I may not have known it in those words, the moment I saw you locked in the pack's cells, but I knew we were headed there."

Silas growled his approval, at the confirmation he'd already thought, felt every time he seated himself inside her there. This woman was meant for him, his one true mate. He didn't give her long, before thrusting into her, causing her to cry out in pleasure. He drew back and did it again and again, pounding deep into her center, finding a steady, heated rhythm, until despite the cold chill in the kitchen air both of them were sweating, heated.

Silas was so rock-hard his balls ached, eager to spend, fill her with his seed. He felt her clench around him as he drew closer and that bit of added pressure and pleasure nearly did him in. "Fuck, I can't hold on much longer, baby." He groaned.

"Don't stop," she pleaded. "Don't stop. Please."

She was right there with him.

Reaching between them, he circled her clit with his fingers, drawing her closer and closer until he gave it an unexpected flick. Cheyenne cried out. She shattered around him, coming apart on a scream as she milked the hot pulses of his cock. Silas swore out his pleasure, every fucking profanity he could think of as his wolf twisted inside him, writhing and alive. He held onto her then, the shudders of her orgasm racking through her as he cradled her in his arms, kissing her with a wild, furious need as he emptied himself inside her.

He kissed any part of her he could get his mouth on.

Her neck, her cheeks, her nose, her lips.

When the last of her orgasm shivered through her, she stared up at him from where he held her, eyes half-lidded and dreamy. He'd finished right alongside her, but he couldn't bring himself to leave her just yet. They stayed locked together like that, two together as one, for several long moments, before Cheyenne brushed a tender hand over the scruff of his beard.

"You think there'll be more pups running around here by next Christmas?" she whispered against his ear.

God, he fucking hoped so, but Silas felt himself stiffen.

It was everything he wanted.

She was everything he wanted.

And yet...

The fact that she'd clearly decided to stay. All they'd done. The way he'd just emptied himself inside her. None of that changed the fact that he wasn't a Grey Wolf in anything more than name only. Never could be. How hadn't he seen that before?

Or maybe he had seen it, and despite that, he'd been just enough of a selfish bastard to take her anyway. He stared down at her, features heavy with a meaning he wasn't certain he could convey in a single look. "I want that more than anything." He dipped his head down to her belly and laid a kiss there, placed his hand against her. "But for your sake, I hope that isn't the case."

11

Cheyenne didn't know what it was she'd said or done that'd caused the moment to go so horribly wrong, but she knew something had changed. One moment Silas had been holding her, laying a gentle kiss to her belly that made her heart flutter both there and in her chest, a kiss so tender and sincere it left her emotions nearly as exposed as the rest of her. But he'd said he loved her, said it first even, and that should have been all that mattered, right?

She eased up on her elbows, where she laid across the kitchen island, watching as he tugged up his jeans and stepped away from her. When he'd told her last night that he wanted her to stay, she'd thought everything had been clear, direct and tailored to her needs. She'd thought when she finally worked up the courage to tell him today that she wanted to stay, that this, *them,* was more important to her than any other plan she'd ever had in place, she'd thought he would be elated, overjoyed even. And he *had* been as he'd claimed her.

Until he wasn't.

She was back to feeling confused, uncertain again.

Silas had pulled on his jacket now, gone out the kitchen's

side door and into the night without another word to her. Going after him was the right thing to do, wasn't it?

But what if he needed space?

Easing her way off the countertop, she tidied herself and the gigantic mess they'd made, allowing enough time that if he needed it, she wouldn't be intruding. She was trying hard to be considerate, attentive to her mate's needs. It didn't come easy to her.

Her mate. Those words thrummed through her.

The thought had once filled her with fear. Fear of being alone. Fear that she'd never have this kind of growing love that'd bloomed between them. But now, the word only filled her with warmth, joy for the future ahead. A future she knew they could both have, if he'd put his own fear aside and let them, let fate be. Be themselves, weird and wild as it was.

She smiled a little at that, silently reclaiming that childhood insult for herself as she pulled on her jacket and headed out into the night.

In the twilight, the towering pines and bare firs of the winter forest blocked the view of the Montana sky, condensing their world until it felt a lot more manageable, small. Like the two of them were the only creatures here, in the soft, quiet sounds of the forest. Silas stood at the clearing edge, near where the cabin's property was nestled among the trees. His back was toward her, but with instincts like his she had no doubt that he heard her soft footfalls in the snow as she approached.

They stood there like that for a long time. Him, looking out into the depths of the forest, like Mother Earth held all the answers to his woes in the wooded palm of her hand, and her watching him, unable to tear her eyes away from this man, this wolf who'd so quickly become the center of her universe, her guiding star.

Finally, when she'd stood alone with him in the silence long enough to make her presence, her quiet support clear, she whispered to him against the howl of the wind. "If I said something wrong, I'm sorry."

Silas whirled around, catching her wrist where she'd reached to touch him in an instant. "Don't talk like that," he whispered back. "You didn't do anything wrong. Not a goddamn thing." He brought his head down and laid a gentle kiss on her gloved fingers. "There's nothing you could do to me that's worse than what I've already done to myself."

Cheyenne shook her head. "I don't understand what you mean." She stepped closer to him then, pressed a hand to his chest. "If you don't want children, it's okay. When you asked me to stay, I just assumed and I-and I started thinking of what things would be like and—"

"I want that more than anything, Cheyenne," he said, cutting her off before she could even fully entertain the thought. "Christmases with you, a family, if that's what you want too. A life shared, even though, just you is more than enough." He shook his head as he took his Stetson off, quickly running his fingers through his hair. "I'm a greedy bastard when it comes to you."

Cheyenne shook her head. "I don't think you're greedy. I wish you wouldn't talk that way about yourself. It isn't fair." The wind whistled through the pine branches in a chorus of winter night air.

"Isn't it?" He placed his Stetson back on his head. "I finally find the one woman I want to spend my life with, standing by my side, but I can't have her all because of the choices I made."

Cheyenne frowned. "Silas, we've already talked about this; you're a Grey Wolf. You swore it, the whole pack saw and—"

"—It's not as simple as that, Cheyenne." He turned toward her then, glancing over his shoulder at her. "Do you know why I didn't want to make the trip to the Missoula pack?"

Cheyenne paused. She hadn't really stopped to consider it. She didn't ruminate on things like that. "Honestly, I didn't much think about it. I tend to take things as they are, but if I had to guess I would have said it was because you didn't want to be stuck with me?" She asked it as a question. But Silas was already shaking his head the moment she finished.

"Not at all. Not by long shot."

"Then why didn't you want to go?"

He placed his hands on the narrow lines of his hips, dipped his head before he looked up at her again. "Because I grew up there. At the Missoula subpack and it was the first time I'd been back to that ranch in fifteen years."

At first, Cheyenne wasn't certain she'd heard him correctly. "What?" She searched his face again, uncertain what she'd find there or if she'd even interpret it accurately if she *could* read it. Man, he was handsome. Painfully beautiful. "But you were a Wild Eight. You're a Grey Wolf now, but . . . "

"I was before too," he said. "Before I joined the Wild Eight."

She'd been young then, a bit younger than him and Missoula was so far. She didn't know every member of the pack and subpacks. Not personally. There were so many of them.

She laughed then. She couldn't help it. "Silas, do you hear yourself? That means you are a Grey Wolf. You always have been too." The truth of that settled into her gut, like the knowledge had always been there. Her pulse raced with the joy of it.

"I was *born* a Grey Wolf," he corrected. "I became a Wild Eight by choice, and I've never regretted it." He shook his head. "Not until you."

Cheyenne felt herself still.

"When I was younger there wasn't a lot of protection for the subpacks. There's been more since Maverick became packmaster but there still isn't . . . " His voice trailed off. "I didn't know what I could do."

She didn't say anything then, instead she stayed silent, listened as she yielded him the space to talk, to heal. The darkness seemed to encroach around them, the shadows growing longer as they stood there. It took a long time, before finally Silas said, "The last Christmas I spent in Missoula, the subpack was set upon by vampires. The first of many attacks to come. My family didn't make it."

When he'd said he was from Missoula, she'd made the connection. There wasn't many from that subpack left, but yet, hearing him confirm it out loud was so much worse. Her heart ached for him. "Silas, I'm so sorry. I—"

"I'm not finished, damn it." He shook his head, held a finger up like if she stopped him, he'd lose his courage and wouldn't be able to say it. "I don't need your pity or theirs." He nodded toward the guest hall, where the other members of her pack would gather to celebrate with all of them once they returned. "I joined the Wild Eight because it wasn't long after that the Seven Range Pact voted to extend their patrol of the vampires."

Cheyenne tried not to lift a brow. "Wouldn't you have wanted that?"

"No. God, you think so much like one of them," he mumbled.

She didn't like the way he said that, like the two of them were different.

They weren't. Not in that way.

He swore under his breath. "The conflict between those bloodsuckers and the pack has gone on ever since. Still is. Don't you see? Where does it start? Where does it end?"

She didn't think he actually wanted her to answer that, but he answered it quickly enough on his own.

"With more wolves buried six feet under, that's where."

She nodded thoughtfully, taking all he said into consideration. "That's why you joined the Wild Eight? Because they were opposed to our pack patrolling the vampires, keeping them in check on behalf of the human hunters?"

He nodded.

He gestured around them, eyes dark and wild. "Here we are fifteen years later. The Wild Eight gone. Hell, Wes is even the second-in-command in your pack and where the hell has that gotten us?" He shook his head. "Just with more lives lost, more blood shed."

"A lot of it was shed at the hands of the Wild Eight," she whispered.

It was a truth neither of them could dispute.

"I know." His eyes filled with regret. "That's why I can't come back to the pack. When the vampires wiped out all of Missoula how do you think they did that?"

Cheyenne froze. "What are you saying?"

"The Wild Eight had already dissolved by then, but where do you think they got the knowledge?"

She understood him clearly then, but she didn't want to, didn't want to consider that the man she loved had done that. Maybe worse.

"You *told* them?" She couldn't keep the fear from her voice, the worry and hurt.

He winced as if she'd struck him. "No. Not directly. But my knowledge of how Missoula ran, knowledge of *your* pack, I shared it with Donnie after Wes left. It was never supposed to go beyond that room, but it did. He passed it to the vamps. How am I supposed to call myself one or your pack again when my choices, my regrets left so many of your packmates for dead. How can I ask anyone to forgive like that?"

Because he wouldn't forgive the vampires for taking the same thing from him. She could see it. He didn't have to say it for her to understand.

"You just do," she whispered, blunt and honest. "You just ask.

It's that simple." She placed a hand on his cheek. "The pack wouldn't have let you join again if they weren't ready to accept you back, to forgive your mistakes, even the big ones. You just have so show them you deserve it."

"But do I?" he asked. "Do I deserve it?" He cupped the sides of her hair in return, drawing her to him as he laid his forehead against hers. "Fuck, I don't deserve you." He growled.

She laid a kiss on his cheek, soft, gentle. "You keep saying that. But repeating it doesn't make it any truer. I can't force you to allow yourself to be happy, Silas. To forgive *yourself*. That's whose forgiveness you need. Not mine or the pack's. You need to see the difference in yourself, the changes you've made. That's only way you're ever really going to heal. You need to find *yourself* worthy, or you're right, you'll never be a member of this pack." She wrapped her arms around him, pulled him close. "But not because I or anyone else don't want you to be."

She kissed him then, a long and deep mingling of tongues until she pulled back and whispered. "Can you try to do that?"

Silas opened his mouth, like he was prepared to answer her. But then she felt his muscles draw tight beneath her hands, coil like a snake prepared to strike. Something rustled in the forest, not far to her right. Cheyenne's heart raced. She didn't think.

"Did you hear that?" she breathed.

Silas nodded once, silently, drawing his blade from where he kept it tucked in his boot. "Cheyenne," he whispered, so low she could hardly hear him.

Her heart was in her throat, pounding with fear. Silas growled, dark eyes flashing to his wolf. "Run to the cabin, lock the door, and don't look back."

12

Cheyenne heeded his warning without question, for which he was grateful, because Silas had all of two seconds before he sensed the vampire breathing at his nape. The bloodsucker slammed into him with supernatural force, knocking him onto the ground. The wind rushed from his lungs in one fell swoop. But he'd expected it. Anticipated it. Silas rolled into the fall, springing back on his feet again just as quick, blade still in hand.

This bloodsucker didn't stand a chance, not with the cold, stormy rage that fueled him. He'd had enough of these bloodsucking fangers fucking with him at Christmas. He snarled.

And yes, he thought Die Hard was, in fact, a Christmas movie. Why did anyone ever ask?

Even if these bloodsuckers had made him hate it for a time.

But he was about to John McClane their ass, so he supposed, he'd let bygones be bygones. With them, himself, and his past. All of it. Cheyenne was right. He needed to forgive, but not forget. He wouldn't lose her over past pack politic.

He swiped his blade, warding off the bloodsucker just long enough so he could shift. A knife may have caused injury for them, harm, enough to give them pause, but only a stake through the heart, decapitation, or his personal favorite, tearing their throats out with his canine teeth truly laid the undead to rest. He took his kills ruthlessly, made it personal.

Cold. Calculated. Fierce.

He shifted into his wolf, legs and limbs seamlessly falling into place until he stood on all four feet, teeth bared, snarling his rage. There was no way this vamp would outpace him now that he stood as his wolf, not when the bloodsucker stood there on two feet, looking for all intents and purposes like a human man, save for the fangs and the pulsing red eyes which tracked his movements through the dark.

Silas bobbed and weaved, barely evading the bloodsucker's speed. But nature would always win when faced against man, dead or alive. If not now, then in the end.

But he wasn't waiting around for that.

He lunged for the bloodsucker, claws tearing into tender flesh as he bit and snarled. The vampire bared its fangs back, hissing and fighting in a swirling blur of hits. And for what? The right to exist? Control these mountainsides? Fuck that.

He and the packmaster needed to have a little discussion about more than a few things.

The vamp gripped him by his scruff, tossing him back. "Your hide is mine, you mangy mutt," the vampire hissed. Silas stiffened. He stood opposite of the fanger, in the snow. He recognized this bloodsucker. That voice. From his Wild Eight days. That realization prickled through him, filling him with awareness, fear for Cheyenne, their packmates.

Their packmates.

His and hers both. She'd helped him understand that now. If they'd have him, he could be both. A former Wild Eight *and* a Grey Wolf. They could be one and the same.

He snarled, advancing again, uncertain he'd live long

enough for Cheyenne to realize exactly how she'd effected him. Made him whole like that.

A single vampire he could handle without so much as blinking an eye. But more?

And there were more. He sensed them.

Scented the sickly sweet scent of death on the breeze.

The one that stood before him would never travel alone. Not against Cillian's orders, their leader. But all the same, when Silas saw his chance, he went for it. He dodged right, faked left, before he lunged again, sinking his canines into the vampire's throat. The iron-filled taste of blood coated his maw, as he ripped and tore, the warm pulse now going still for a final time on his tongue. He shifted back to human form in an instant. Blood coated his front as he snatched his blade from the snow in preparation for the coming onslaught.

He spat a mouthful of blood into the snow and dirt. His teeth would be stained red.

"Silas!" Cheyenne's shout drew his attention to his left, echoing in his ears.

His gaze darted in her direction just in time to see her shift into her wolf, along with several other of the younger alpha warriors of the Grey Wolf pack. He growled his disapproval from across the clearing as she bounded toward him, but she snarled back, where she now stood in wolf form. She hadn't listened to him and locked herself inside. She'd gone for help.

He couldn't have been prouder of her. Furious? Sure. Terrified? Yes. Feeling far too protective of her? Definitely. But proud all the same. She was tender hearted as she was fierce, brave. A cacophony of growls filled his ears. The snarls of the Grey Wolves. The approach of the vampire's onslaught as they hissed. The moon hung in the sky overhead, staring down at them and illuminating the snow in its glittering light.

With this few wolves and so many bloodsuckers, they'd die

out here, become nothing more than food for the dirt and snow beneath their feet. Blood fodder as the vampires bled them.

He didn't want that to happen. Didn't want them to be over yet, before they'd even really had a chance to begin. But he'd feared this from the moment they'd returned to find the ranch unguarded. He'd hoped he could spare Cheyenne if they came, of course, protect her. Yet it was too late for that. They were surrounded, but she was there now, beside him, prepared for battle, as kind and full hearted as she was wild. His beautiful glorious mate.

Silas turned toward her, prepared to tell her he loved her one last time. "I love you," he whispered. In wolf form, she couldn't answer back. But the echo across the mountainside did.

He hadn't counted on that, the whole of the Grey Wolf pack, returned early, exactly as they'd left. A shiver coursed down Silas' spine as the sound of Maverick and the other wolves' howls filled his ears, echoing out into the night. From where she stood beside him on all four paws, Cheyenne's golden eyes met his. He smirked at that and together they threw back their heads and howled, the haunting sound of the pack all together as one filling the mountainside.

A fierce, echoing warning to their enemies that the strength of the wolf was its pack.

The other Grey Wolf warriors burst forth from the forest, the whole of their kind circling and working together as one to ease the vampires back. The bloodsuckers weren't stupid. They'd come prepared for no more than a handful of wolves, only intending to catch the stragglers left in the days before their return, so the bloodsuckers fled. Quickly. Chased into the night.

A Christmas fucking miracle.

With the immediate threat receding, shouts from the pack's elite warriors followed, orders to get Wolf Pack Run's perimeter secured. But Silas couldn't bring himself to pay attention, he was too busy watching the naked woman now standing at his side, her eyes the blazing gold of her wolf like the hopeful glitter of a Christmas ornament.

She launched herself into his arms then, wrapping her own around his neck.

"I told you to stay inside," he grumbled against her ear, before he buried his face in the crook of her neck, the soft tendrils of her hair.

"You really thought I'd listen to that?" She swatted at his arm, playfully. "When you'd been going on with all that foolish nonsense about how you're not one of us?" She shook her head. "I'd never leave you like that. To fight alone."

They stayed like that for a long time, wrapped up in one another, seemingly unaware of everything, everyone around them, until from behind them, they heard the familiar sound of the packmaster clearing his throat.

Silas turned facing the Grey Wolf leader, Cheyenne shamelessly in his arms. Maverick glanced between them, eyeing them a bit like the cat that'd caught the canary rather than a packmaster, a powerful wolf who'd caught his former enemy embracing one of his pack's most beloved she-wolves. "I guess this means I win the bet."

From behind him, Wes cursed, as his brother, the Grey Wolf high commander, Colt Cavanaugh let out a victorious whoop.

Silas snarled, lip curled. "What the fuck does that mean?"

From nearby, Wes huffed his annoyance. "We all had a bet going to see if you and Cheyenne would *finally* get together by the time we got back." He sauntered toward them. "Cheyenne didn't know, of course."

Silas glanced down at the woman in his arms, and she nodded her head in confirmation.

"We didn't figure it'd take the two of you this long after she let you out of the cells," Maverick shrugged. "My bet was for when you got back from Missoula."

Silas glanced between the two men and the handful of the other elite warriors alongside their mates who had crowded around them now, exchanging pleased glances.

Silas stammered. "But . . . but you fucking told me to take care of her? And I . . . and we . . . " He'd never been at more of a loss of words in his life.

"Take care of her?" Maverick's brow furrowed momentarily until he threw back his head and laughed. "You thought I meant Cheyenne?" That deep-throated chuckle could only be rivaled by Santa alone. "I meant my truck, you fool."

His truck?

Silas stilled, remembering how the packmaster had tossed him his keys the moment after he'd said that.

"The Grey Wolves females can handle themselves, Silas." Wes clapped him on the arm. "Best get with the program."

"But what about the trust test?" he spat, mind reeling. He was still trying to piece together the part where they'd taken bets on him sleeping with one of their most cherished she-wolves. Like they were amused—no, *pleased* about the idea of seeing them together.

Like he was *one* of them. A part of their pack.

"Serving the pack as you were asked, looking out for their best interest when you returned, *that* was your trust test," Maverick said. "Not protecting Cheyenne. She's more than capable of handling herself."

"Amen to that." Cheyenne grinned more than a little, preening really.

Of course, she was, but he'd thought . . .

Fuck, he didn't know what sort of ridiculous nonsense he'd been thinking. That because she was sweet, tender-hearted that meant she wasn't an accomplished warrior? Somehow, he'd forgotten that. The only thing he knew was that he loved her, and now, she loved him back and somehow in the midst of all this insanity about packs, and loyalties, and futures, and Christmas, and pack politics, they were going to figure out a way to make it work.

"And the pack?" Silas asked. "They still don't trust me, even if *you* do." He frowned. He was still trying to wrap his head around that.

Maverick shrugged. "Well, I suppose they'll have to get over it, considering you'll likely be the father of one of them in roughly," Maverick sniffed, "nine months from now?" The Grey Wolf packmaster chuckled.

Cheyenne nestled against his side, blushing a little at that, but she seemed far more used to the idea of her packmates being far too aware of the intimate business of her life than he was.

He wasn't certain he'd ever get used to it.

"Merry Christmas, Silas. Welcome to the pack." Maverick grinned, as he and the other warriors made their way across the mountainside, finishing their work of securing the ranch border. Silas wanted to discuss a bit more with him about that, about security and this whole warring-with-vampires business, but right now, he didn't have time for his past.

Not when he had a whole wide future to unfold.

He turned toward Cheyenne, watching her stand there before him, nose red from the cold. Without warning, he swept her into his arms, pulling her close. "Let's get you inside," he grumbled against her cheek.

She wagged a finger at him. "Oh no. Not before you answer me something. I heard the way you demanded I stay inside. Don't think you're not going to hear more about *that* later."

"Mhmmm," Silas purred against her skin. "And what do I need to do to make amends?"

"Promise me that every Christmas, I still get to lay claim to my chair." She wiggled closer to him. "We'll play Santa in it." She gave him a way too obvious wink, and he laughed.

"I think I can do you better." He brushed a strand of her hair back from her face, tucked it behind one of her pert little ears. "What do you think of sharing my bed for forever? Being my mate?"

"I've been waiting all season to hear you say that." She kissed him, then, sighing against his mouth a little. "And one more question," she whispered feverishly against his lips, cupping both his cheeks in her hands.

"What's that?" he growled, quickly losing his patience. All he wanted to do was get her alone again, undress her and maybe grab some more of that peppermint frosting. Now that he knew they had all the time in the world, a future ahead to explore and love and do way more of that.

"Do you still hate Christmas?" She nuzzled her head against him.

Silas grumbled a little. Even for him, it was hard not to smile when she was cuddling him like that. "Maybe," he grumped.

Cheyenne smiled that sunshiny grin at him, hitting him full force with that joyous again as she let out a pleased giggle. "We'll keep working on it."

He smiled at her then, carrying her back inside where the warmth of the cabin and the fire waited for them beside the glittering tree. "I'll look forward to that."

SERIES NOTE

Thank you so much for reading *Cowboy Wolf Christmas*! I hope you enjoyed the ride!

While *Cowboy Wolf Christmas* stands on its own, it's set in the world of the Seven Range Shifters, and chronologically this story takes place between the events of the fourth and fifth series volumes, *Fierce Cowboy Wolf* and *Wild Cowboy Wolf*.

ABOUT THE AUTHOR

Kait Ballenger is the award-winning author of the Seven Range Shifter and Rogue Brotherhood paranormal romance series, where she weaves captivating tales filled with dark, sexy alpha heroes and the independent women who bring them to their knees.

When Kait's not preoccupied writing "intense and riveting" paranormal plots or "high-voltage" love scenes that make even seasoned romance readers blush, she can usually be found spending time with her family or with her nose buried in a good book. She lives in Florida with her husband and two sons.

Readers can visit Kait's website and sign up for her newsletter at www.kaitballenger.com.

For right inquiries, contact Nicole Resciniti at The Seymour Agency: nicole@theseymouragency.com

ACKNOWLEDGMENTS

First, thank you to Asa Maria Bradley and the other Shifter Sisters for including me in the Shifter and Mistletoe anthology in which this novella originally appeared. I feel so fortunate to have collaborated with such a talented group of authors.

Next, thanks must go to my husband, Jon, who is always my first reader. He gets the chapters hot off the press and is always enthusiastic in his support.

Last, but certainly not least, a huge thank you to Mara Wells, who not only helped me brainstorm the idea for this story, but who served as a sharp editor on a tight deadline. Mara, I couldn't ask for a more loyal friend or a more skilled critique partner—thank you! I'm so grateful to have you in my life.

ALSO BY KAIT BALLENGER

Seven Range Shifters

Cowboy Wolf Trouble

Cowboy in Wolf's Clothing

Wicked Cowboy Wolf

Fierce Cowboy Wolf

Wild Cowboy Wolf

Cowboy Wolf Outlaw

The Rogue Brotherhood

Rogue Wolf Hunter

ALSO BY KAIT BALLENGER

Sage Range Shifters

Cowboy Wolf Trouble
Cowboy in Wolf's Clothing
Wicked Cowboy Wolf
Rogue Cowboy Wolf
Wild Cowboy Wolf
Cowboy Wolf Outlaw

The Rogue Brotherhood

Rogue Wolf Rising